CHINCOTEAGUE
BUGS

Paul Tait Roberts

Bohannon Book Ranch

Chincoteague Bugs
Paul Tait Roberts

© 2021 Paul Tait Roberts

All rights reserved. No part of this publication may be reproduced, stored in a retrieval system or transmited in any form or by any means, electronic, mechanical, photocopying, recording or otherwise without the prior permision of the publisher or in accordance with the provisions of the Copyright, Designs and Patents Act 1988 or under the terms of any licence permitting limited copying issued by the Copyright Licensing Angency.

Published by:
Bohannon Book Ranch
Powhatan, 23139 VA, USA

Typesetting: Paul Roberts

Cover Design: Paul Roberts

A CIP record for this book is available from the Library of Congress Cataloging-in-Publication Data

ISBN-13: 979 8 71113 141 0

Printed in USA find the easter eggs within this book

A true story

about myths we embrace

and truths we conveniently ignore.

Somewhere a ukelele plays:

Chincoteague Bugs

There. On the end of my nose. The little fella ain't much bigger than a pore. I could just have easily not noticed him had my eyes focused an inch beyond. It's not so hard to see something so close and so obvious if one chooses to, it's just that, one often doesn't choose to. And instead of seeing something as it is, we look elsewhere for that something we'd rather see. That's when a little fella like this bites, and draws blood. Ow! Like that. If I leave him alone, he continues to aggrieve me and I'll have a big red welt as a result. If I swat him, I hit myself in the face. A dilemma I brought upon myself. Now I'm forced to deal with him. I smush him, leaving a bloody mess so close and so obvious it's not hard to see, though I still choose not to see it. It's just a little red spot, but to curious onlookers who choose to focus beyond the end of their own noses, it's a ghastly blemish. Maybe they're helpful, and point at my nose saying, "you've got a little something there...," Maybe they don't want to embarrass me, and they say nothing, and I walk around all day with an coagulant splotch in the center of my face, all because, someone else also chose not to see it.

Had I had any interest in this little fella, I could have understood him better, why he was there, and what he was doing. Since my attention was elsewhere, I know nothing of his story, or the story of others like him. And this is how it goes...

About halfway up the right side of America, where ocean waves splash ashore and push froth up yellow sand beaches, you'll find the state of Virginia. On the right hand side of Virginia, where a sizable amount of froth gets pushed up onto the beach, you'll find an elongated peninsula standing on its tippy-tip: the Delmarva peninsula. This strip of land is divvied up with imaginary dotted lines by three states who care about the importance of these dotted lines; Delaware, Maryland, and Virginia: and so there you have, Delmarva. Part-way up the Delmarva just below an imaginary dotted line made by those who care, is the end of Virginia, in that particular direction. There, you'll find a foolishly named government airport where very smart people shoot large pointy tubes into space. In the upper right hand corner of that airport is a building that contains an office, a desk, an outdated computer, a dull gray stapler, and a plastic phone. To the right of the phone you'll find a NASA engineer who ponders the significance of the universe, but who is wholly unable to quantify the magnitude of his own ignorance. Outside and to the right of the engineer's office you'll find a highly polished silver Beechcraft 18, a polished art deco era twin engine airplane lifting off the runway and departing over a wide, shallow channel of water: Queen Sound Channel. To the right of that channel of water, you'll find an island and its inhabitants over which the Beech 18 sprays poison. They call this island, Chincoteague. To the right of

Chincoteague, in the uppermost right hand corner of Virginia is another island, Assateague, which is the northeastern-most place in Virginia where the ocean pushes froth up onto the beach. No one wants to live there, except wild animals, which is why they call it a wildlife refuge. The Beech 18, doesn't spray poison on this island, since the only inhabitants there are the wild animals, and bugs, and the latter especially, pay no taxes to subsidize their own genocide.

So, the Beech 18 makes a u-turn before Assateague and it then showers yet another round of poison over Chincoteague, often traversing the part of town where you'll find Don's Seafood Restaurant—listen, there goes the plane right now. Inside that restaurant is the upstairs dining room where you'll find a pretty and punky, tatted, young waitress who hankers to be anywhere, but where she currently is. To the right of the dining room, in the bar, between the whiskey shelf and a stack of high chairs, you'll find a microphone on a stand, a stool, a ukelele, and me. But you already know that, since you're sitting right there in front of me at your table, sipping your Old Fashions, and your Martinis, and your brown ales, just to pass the time. I'm here to help you do just that.

I'm a storyteller, and I always tell the truth--except when I don't. Now if you look to the right, out the window and over at the Queen Sound Channel, you'll find the unhealed scars left by an ancient cataclysm. It's actually a gaping wound, filled with water. It festered for millennia and infected our history, changing everything, and is still influencing us today.

Believe me—if you find me believable. I'm the one human on this planet that understands the incomprehensible events that occurred here, in the upper right hand corner of Virginia. Believe me when I say I am the one human on this planet credible enough to retell this not-so-tall tale that predates human intelligence, and perseveres into modern times. Believe me, because I am an authority on this matter, even though I am, at the same time, completely unable to answer the question "why are there high-chairs stacked *in the bar* at Don's Seafood Restaurant?"

Molly Rowley abhorred her life. Her father was a fry cook at the Burger Chef, because that was the best job he could get on the Delmarva with his stunted education and skills. As a teen, Molly watched her Dad humiliate himself every day by donning a brown, red and yellow polyester uniform and hat that made him look like a walking hamburger. She saw him come home late at night, bedraggled and spent. His forehead and face coated with a fine sheen of french fry grease, forming a breeding ground for the next day's zits. He looked completely demoralized after each shift, his manhood stolen from him by a dead end job. Molly was determined to avoid this fate.

    Lucas, her boyfriend, seemed to be the way out. Molly first caught sight of Lucas in high school as he swaggered down the hallways in expensive-looking cowboy boots, black jeans and chrome studded black jean jacket. He was one of the few guys in high school who could grow a full beard, and did. His lank hair dangled around his shoulders and his musky, unwashed aroma assured everyone within smelling distance that he didn't care about anything, except when he did. Molly couldn't resist his charm. She found him exotic and dangerous, and the very sight of him excited her.

    Late one Friday night, Molly's Dad came home from work exhausted and beaten down, as usual. This is when he first met Lucas, who currently was making out with his daughter on the living room couch. He immediately disliked the boy. Molly's Dad dragged the upstart from the couch, out through the front door, and across the front lawn to show him that the road that led to his house also led away from his house. Molly bellowed and screamed in protest, tears streaking down her cheeks all the while. Once her Dad's foot met Lucas' backside, he turned to Molly and explained, "You won't go anywhere with that punk." Molly's Dad had a remarkable insight into Lucas' character. He knew full well that Lucas was destined to be a fry cook at the Burger Chef, or worse, because Lucas was a mirror image of his own younger self.

But Molly heard her Dad's words differently, especially the word, "punk." She liked this word. It was as exotic as Lucas, and so therefore, fitting and desirable.

By the next afternoon Molly powdered her face white, dragging electric-red lipstick across her mouth, applying mascara with an industrial bristle brush and spreading cerulean eye shadow on her lids with an icing knife. She looked into the mirror and upon seeing that she was incomplete, dashed down to the pharmacy for some hair dye. Back home, she locked herself in the bathroom and soaked her hair in chemicals over and over again, until it was so unnaturally black even light couldn't escape. The next day she presented her new look to everyone at school, which to Molly, was coming out to the world. In public, people on the Delmarva gave Molly a once or twice over, and labeled her "that punk girl." More culturally aware and less provincial people would see her as "Goth," a Tim Burton ashen faced girl-waif. Molly saw herself differently. She looked into the mirror and saw her transformation as an escape from the mundane, and a path to a world of possibilities.

Within a few days, Lucas arrived at school with "Molly" tattooed on his forearm. Molly inherently understood that she would soon return the favor. Molly and Lucas then began an unwitting race to "out-tattoo" each other, spending a whole lot of money that neither had in order to get a little bit of ink here, and a little bit of ink there. Molly soon realized that her arms were fully sleeved, and in general, her skin had become a overcrowded canvas. So, she chose to put a new tattoo on the only vacant real estate she could find: the side of her neck. The next time Lucas saw Molly, she flaunted a large dragon-blue spider web spanning from her right collarbone, up the side of her neck, to just short of her right ear lobe. Lucas rhapsodized about its symbolism, "It's beautiful, like you, but like you, it can capture and devour a soul. It says I'm a work of graceful, subtle art, but I can also be venomous." This assessment surprised Molly, who got the tattoo solely because she thought it looked neat. Nevertheless she embraced the symbolism, and ramped up her rebellious nature, defying Dad, and defying the world.

School in particular, did nothing for her anymore. Her patience ran out during the very middle of Monday math class, where she grew so desperately bored, that she stood up and left the room mid lecture, sauntered down the hall, threw open the exit and flashed a middle finger over her shoulder at the institution though no actual people were present to witness this final gesture. Molly felt good. She felt free. The world was hers and she would explore it now, on her own terms.

    An unimaginably long time ago, our oversized salamander-like ancestors peeked their heads above the ocean water. They then peeked above the surface of rivers and creeks where they spotted what they thought might be food on what we today would call "land." They had no word for "land." They only knew that their grumbling, underfed tummies urged them to pull themselves out of the water, and flop themselves up on "land" to get something to eat, which they did. Once there, had they bothered to look up, they would have noticed some very unusual things happening in the sky. But, our oversized salamander-like ancestors were plainly too dumb to understand the concept of "the sky." They had no word for "sky" either, and without the word "sky," it didn't exist to them, so, they had no reason to look up. They were just too dumb to think beyond their stomachs, and food was right there in front of them, so they ate it, much like today's humans.

    If they had looked up, they still would not have been smart enough to understand what was happening in low Earth orbit. There, space curved upon itself infinitely, forming a sphere of refracted light that warped and distorted the view of the stars. It looked like a crystal ball floating over the planet. But unlike a crystal ball there was no surface to speak of. Had one of our oversized salamander-like ancestors tried to touch this sphere, they would've seen their flipper-like foot stretch toward infinity, and appear on the other side of the universe. Had they been smart enough, they would have then and there, changed Earth's evolutionary history by discovering the wormhole. But instead, they were occupied by hunger, chewing grass on a river bank.

A wormhole can be any size. Why not? This wormhole was about the size of a basketball. In this case, that's all it needed to be, because the wormhole was a little larger than the size of a star cruiser that emerged from it. The star cruiser itself was a sphere about the size of a basketball. Its glossy metal surface was pristinely smooth and partitioned by black longitudinal lines running from pole to pole, which made it look even more like a basketball. This was a Moss-Skweeto mother-ship: a vessel of exploration and scientific discovery.

Now, earlier, I sang about Chincoteague bugs, but what they really are, is, Moss-Skweetos. Bugs is just easier to say over and over, or in rapid succession, or even by itself, when you compare it to saying Moss-Skweetos, even though that's the correct word to describe them.

Now, it so happens, that the engineers on the mother ship miscalculated the span of time they would need to keep the wormhole open in order to safely pass the ship through to the other side of the universe. So as the last section of the mother-ship exited the wormhole, the wormhole quickly collapsed, leaving part of the ship behind, on the other side of the universe. Moss-Skweeto crew members on those decks died, of course, but vital ship operating systems were also lost, especially the inertial dampeners, what we would today call "the brakes."

Without its brakes, the mother-ship hurtled uncontrollably toward the Earth. It became a fireball in the atmosphere, scorching the gleaming metal hull. Had our oversized salamander-like ancestors looked up, they would have seen a trail of blue-green hot plasma streaking across the sky, but instead they were pooping out the grass they had previously eaten. The earth filled the view screens on the mother-ship's bridge and the ship's officers made the emergency call, "brace for impact."

The star cruiser hurtled over the planet at hypersonic speeds. It streaked out of the sky. The plasma degenerated into black, sooty smoke. The mother-ship strafed whole forests vaporizing treetops. In one last ditch effort to save the ship and crew, the Moss-Skweeto pilots heroically pulled back on the controls, flaring the descent rate. But the ship crashed across a narrow strip of land, an isthmus, digging a deep, long ditch, nearly bisecting it. The star cruiser came to rest, smoldering and half buried in sand and silt. The Moss-Skweeto ship stopped inches short of cutting completely through the isthmus, where the entire ship's inhabitants would have certainly drowned underneath the whitecaps of an adjacent saltwater bay.

A hatch burst open on one side of the star cruiser. Moss-Skweetos, scared, tired and injured, fluttered out to assess their situation. They looked up at the blue sky (they had a word for sky, so they knew to look up). It was strangely different from their blood-red sky back home. They surveyed the crash site; the long ditch and the black silt and yellow sand churned up by their mother-ship. They tended their wounds and implemented survival directives, the first of which was to reopen the wormhole and send an emergency signal back to the home world, to initiate a rescue. But the ship was mostly destroyed, and they discovered that their technologies were beyond repair. They would have to take advantage of the Earth's resources, salvage what little was left on the ship, and develop new ways to call home.

It was at that point that one of our oversized salamander-like ancestors noticed a tuft of grass on the shore. He crawled out of the water and flopped himself onto the land. He flopped again, and again until he was finally able to take a bite of grass. Had he been smart enough, he would have noticed a long, wide scorched ditch on the other side of the grass. Had he not been so dumb, he would have seen that this freshly dug ditch led straight to this tuft of grass that he was about to eat. Had he been curious enough, he would have focused six inches beyond the tuft of grass and discovered an alien race and their mother-ship lodged within the exposed roots of the grass. But, he was plainly too dumb to think beyond his stomach. So, he chomped on the tuft of grass and yanked and yanked and yanked until he uprooted the whole thing, creating a gap in the shore. Sand poured into the gap like an hourglass, and then more poured in, burying the mother-ship. Our oversized salamander-like ancestor blithely ate his lunch as the land around him collapsed into the ditch and as salt water from the bay rushed in, forcing the Moss-Skweetos to take wing, flying away with just their lives intact. They watched in horror and despair, and to no avail, as the ditch flooded, destroying the last remnants of their ship, their society, and their dignity. They helplessly watched as this stupid creature made survival exponentially harder for them. The creature obliviously slinked into the new waterway, like it had always been there, looking for something else to eat.

This ditch, is what we now call Queen Sound Channel. And this is how Chincoteague peninsula, became Chincoteague Island.

    As a kid, Darryl Baker was more than sure that he wanted to be an etymologist. But he reached high school and he began to understand that words mean stuff, and that etymology was the study of exactly that. That wasn't what he wanted to do. So now understanding just enough about word origins, and especially word spelling, Darryl took the word etymologist, and added the letter "n." He then changed the "y" to an "o" and before him, on paper, was his real life calling, an entomologist, the zoological study of bugs. Who, Darryl wondered, would invent such similar words for such different things, surely not an etymologist, he thought.

    Darryl loved bugs, as many kids do. At first he picked them up with a stick and watched them amble down its length, and then back again after he flipped the stick over. He caught lightning bugs and collected them in a jar, only to realize that their glowing abdomens progressively dimmed if air-holes weren't poked into the lid. He caught katydids, grasshoppers and praying mantises. At first he drew pictures of them with crayons, and later he catalogued them all with his Kodak 110 Pocket Instamatic. He couldn't get enough of bugs—until he could. Traipsing through the woods behind his house one day, he noticed movement on the ground amongst a bed of fallen leaves. Darryl bent over for a closer look. He learned then and there what many entomologists already knew: yellow jackets sting only when you invade their nest.

Over the course of the next week, the stings over most of his face and body were terribly slow to heal. Darryl sat outside on his parent's back patio at night, because a cool evening breeze felt good on his wounds. He sat in a cheap lounge chair, sore, and sullen. His mother had treated each welt with a homespun baking soda paste, which made Darryl feel like a white polka dotted idiot. He gingerly leaned back onto the lounge chair and stared into the sky, longing for a respite of any sort. That night he realized the sky was so dark and clear that he could make out the Milky-Way. He pondered its significance, and his place in the universe. He then pondered other people's place in the universe: people on Earth, and then, people not on Earth. His welts itched and he scratched and squirmed in the lounge chair. "Screw bugs," he whispered. He looked back at the stars and proclaimed, "I'm going to be an astrologer!" That is, until he later realized again that words mean stuff, and that the word he was looking for was astronomer. He didn't want to write horoscopes in the newspaper, but instead, Darryl wanted to devote his life to discovering Extra Terrestrial life.

Astronomy, unlike entomology, treated Darryl well throughout high school, so much so that he pursued a high minded degree in college about the high altitudes of space. The cosmos fascinated him endlessly, and he eventually earned a master's degree, and then a PhD, for which he created and successfully defended his dissertation: *The probable existence of intelligent and evolved life on other planets, and the improbability of Earthly inhabitants to ever get actual proof of Extra Terrestrial existence.*

Darryl mastered critical thought in the academic world, and he effectively navigated the required processes to earn multiple degrees, walking off the graduation platform with a self-satisfied smile on his face, and a proxy diploma in his hand. As he walked off the graduation stage, Darryl, like every other college graduate throughout history, believed that his talents would be immediately recognized by a large, important organization or corporation, that would then scoop him up, give him an office with large windows, a real wood desk, an obscenely colossal salary, a dental plan, and a month's paid vacation to boot.

But over the next several months Darryl developed an understanding every college graduate in history develops: this scenario wasn't going to happen.

Darryl, therefore, put his feet to the street and knocked on doors and made cold calls in search of a job: any job. He brought his impressive collegiate resume, and showed his credentials to the manager of the pizza delivery store, the grocery store, the big box store, and the burrito store, to name a few. Each and every time, the manager chuckled under his breath, and then flatly rejected Darryl because he was way too smart to deliver a pizza, or to make a burrito. And though Darryl truly was smart enough to calculate the mass of a black hole and its gravitational effect on time, he was only now beginning to understand that the academic world is not very good at preparing a person for life outside the academic world.

Dejected and forlorn, Darryl found himself wandering into a Cuban-styled cigar bar for a drink. The place was called Havanna '59. It was clearly named after January 1st, 1959, the date Fidel

Castro's Cuban Revolution officially ended, which ousted President Fulgencio Batista, and replaced his government with a socialist state. What is unclear is whether the name Havanna '59 is a reverential nod to Castro's socialist success, whether it's a rueful mourning for Batista's capitalist downfall, or whether it's just a cheap ploy to sell cigars, none of which actually come from embargoed Cuba.

Darryl sat at the bar nursing the cheapest whisky available. As his glass approached half empty, an argument developed at the far end of the bar. A lady was furiously chewing out a bar-back, though her voice never got any louder than a whisper. She evidently didn't want to upset the clientele by shouting, even though she was perfectly happy to carry out an angry argument in front of them. Darryl figured correctly that she was the boss. She pointed fingers around the room and back at the bar-back, who pointed back at her. Their faces reddened and veins nearly popped out of their respective necks as they continued to whisper-yell at each other. The bartender pretended not to notice by wiping down the counter and diligently filling more drink orders. Darryl couldn't help but be interested. Eventually the bar-back crossed his arms and grimaced. He knew he had lost the argument, until that is, he found he had one more card to play against the cranky boss: he took off his apron, threw it on the floor, and stormed out. The bartender passed by and Darryl grabbed his attention, "Are you hiring?"

"If that's what you want," the bartender shrugged, and he then walked over to talk with the boss lady.

Darryl reached into his blazer pocket to retrieve his resume, but then thought better of it. The bartender conferred with the boss, who looked over her shoulder at Darryl. She nodded, and that was that.

Now let's get something straight before we move on, it ain't Chink o' Teeg. You don't ch, ch, chop it, you sh, sh, shop it: Shink. And you don't teeg it, you tig it, dig it? Shink-uh-tig. The pronunciation of the names of lots of places on this planet are debatable, sometimes hotly debatable. For instance, some folks versed in the etymology and pronunciation of Spanish derived words, might call a certain town in the mountains of Virginia, Buena Vista (Bwayna Vista), while others, especially those in the mountains of Virginia, are dead sure that it's Byoo-na Vista. What you say, and how you say it, largely depends on who you are and what part of the planet you're from. But the name of this island that lies under the foundation of Don's Seafood Restaurant, is what I say it is. And even though many folks will say that I'm wrong, which I almost certainly am, it is simply not debatable within the pages of this story. Mostly because I like to shink, and I like to tig, whatever those two words mean. Now, all of this is made even more confusing because of how you address Shink uh' tig's sister island, Ass-a-teeg. The first part of this name is of course as you might think it ought to be said. So is the middle. But the end ain't a tig, it's a teeg. Tea is sweet on Assateague. See?

    When white guys first came to this area, they spotted this island and knew immediately what it meant: waterfront property! They turned to the local Indians who lived on the Delmarva, a tribe known as the Gincoteague. The white guys asked if they could buy the island from the tribe. The Indians glanced across Queen Sound Channel at the island. They understood that a plague of flesh eating bugs lived over there, but kept that fact to themselves. They shrugged, said, "Sure," and sold the island for a song. The white guys moved in, named the island after the tribe, but promptly screwed up the name Gincoteague, because they too preferred to shink and to tig.

The very instant the white guys stepped onto the island's shores they began swatting the air, their faces, and their arms. They had immediately discovered their new Moss-Skweeto neighbors. And though the white guys were constantly tortured and attacked by the bugs, they somehow managed to tolerate them and co-habitate with them on the island. This is probably because they understood that the words "waterfront property" were often translatable into the word "money." And though prospective buyers of this property would nearly be eaten alive by the bugs, the early white guys on Chincoteague also knew they couldn't get rid of the bugs, since neither insecticides, nor their delivery systems, had been yet conceived of. They didn't even have words for these things. So, they turned a blind eye to the bugs' adverse affect on the value of their land and their economy.

Oddly enough though, they weren't willing to turn a blind eye on what they perceived to be the Gincoteague tribe's adverse affect on the value of their land and their economy. They believed that if brown people were in the area, specifically, the brown people who sold them the waterfront property for a song, people who mostly kept to themselves on the Delmarva, their very presence would deter other white guys from coming to Chincoteague to spend their money. The Gincoteague, therefore, had to go.

Even though the early white guys couldn't get rid of the bugs, they found that they could get rid of the Indians, and so they did. But in honor of those noble Indians they had just dispersed and essentially erased from the map of the upper right hand corner of Virginia, they left the name of the island as-is, even though it was the wrong name.

Five years after dropping out of high school, Molly sat with her boyfriend Lucas on a rented couch, inside their rented single-wide trailer, on a swampy lot on the Delmarva. Both stopped getting tattoos, because neither had any place left to put one, nor could they really afford to pay for tattoos, much less for their rented couch or trailer. Lucas, one of those guys who in high school could grow a full beard, and did, was also one of those guys who had a shiny bald dome by his early twenties. Every day he would humiliate himself by donning a brown, red and yellow polyester uniform and hat that made him look like a walking hamburger. He then went to work for Molly's Dad, who was now the manager at the Burger Chef.

Molly, who spent her teenage years dreading the mundane life her Dad lived, trapped in a low wage job leading to exactly nowhere, found herself rejected again and again as an under-qualified high school dropout who applied for every mundane job she could find on the Delmarva. One morning, fed up with failure, she found herself driving her rusty two hundred dollar Plymouth K car across a causeway that connected the Delmarva to Chincoteague Island. She didn't know what she was doing, or where she was going, or why. She just had to get out of the trailer, away from Lucas, and away from the tedium of doing nothing.

Molly parked her car downtown and meandered up and down the sidewalks. She mostly kept to herself, looking down at her feet, trying not to look at other people, especially tourists, who all seemed to have what she didn't have: money, and the freedom that goes with having it. She soon found herself taking in the shade under the crayon-blue awning of Don's Seafood Restaurant. She felt a twinge on her spiderweb tattoo, and absentmindedly swatted a bug that bit her neck. Molly leaned a shoulder against Don's huge plate glass front window and stared inside. The place was teeming with tourists and locals alike, all of whom were stuffing their faces with seafood. They happily gorged themselves, never noticing Molly languishing out front, sizing them up.

Now, you and I already know what Molly instinctively deduced at that moment: seafood is pricey. She zeroed in on an older couple sitting by the salad bar. Molly watched the old man stuff his face with deviled crab, and the old lady gulp down a raw oyster. She knew that not long afterwards, that old man or old lady would pass a credit card, or cash, to the waitress in order to pay a substantial bill. Molly also knew that substantial bills were often accompanied by substantial tips. Molly sidled down the length of the window and walked inside the main entrance. She stopped at the "please wait to be seated" sign and awkwardly, uncomfortably, stood there. The hostess caught sight of Molly, grabbed a menu and utensils wrapped in a paper napkin and approached her.

"One for lunch?" she asked.

Molly replied, "Are you hiring?"

Over the last millennia of Earth's history, the bugs witnessed early humans grab the leg bones of their last meal and smack them together. Early humans realized that this made a sound and before they knew it they were smacking the bones together over and over in time. Other humans around the proverbial campfire, unable to contain themselves by this new sound, leapt to their feet, hopped and squatted, flailed their arms about and kicked their feet in the air, usually at nothing.

A short time later, by evolutionary standards, early humans stretched animal hides over bones and carved out tree trunks to make drums, and hollowed out other bones to create primitive flutes. As the millennia progressed, so did the sounds created by humans. The bugs watched from a distance over a long, long time as clicks and booms and toots transformed into the sublime compositions of Bach, Mozart, Beethoven, and eventually Zappa.

Humans, smugly patted themselves on the back, because they had invented and developed the greatest achievement in the universe: music. Only, they hadn't.

While humans were still paramecium in a raindrop, Moss-Skweetos on the home world congregated on the trunk of a tree, where they joined legs, proboscises and abdomens with each other, forming a net of bugs encompassing the body of the plant. They beat their wings and pulsated their bodies in waves that swept from bug to bug. The bark of the tree oscillated, sending vibrations across the rings, deep into the wooden core where it propagated all the way to the tippy-tips of the branches and leaves, spawning beautiful cantatas and symphonies. From the leaves the music undulated the air, creating waves of sound, traveling anywhere on the globe, for every Moss-Skweeto to hear. It became an elegant form of communication across the planet, and eventually into space.

The bugs looked at the humans and their music, and thought how quaint it was that the humans would consider, even for a moment, that amongst the endless planets, within the endless galaxies, within the infinite universe, that they, with their gumdrop-sized imaginations, could possibly be the only creators of music.

The humans took their hubris a step further, believing that they had created some of the greatest musical instruments conceivable; the Stradivarius, the Steinway, the Les Paul. The bugs, by the way, disapproved of these instruments, because they believed live trees made better music.

And though the Stradivarius, the Steinway, and the Les Paul have certainly produced many tingling goosebump moments on the arms of millions of people, I've always considered them inferior to the most significant musical instrument made by man: the kazoo. Anyone can pick up a kazoo, lift it to their lips, start humming, and become a maestro in just seconds. If we took the time it takes to master a kazoo, and actually listen to the bugs singing around us instead of swatting them, we would know that coincidentally, a kazoo makes the exact sound of a group of singing Moss-Skweetos.

And while we were still paramecium in a raindrop, the bugs had been singing this song for generations:

Bazoopa zoop zoop

zoopa zoop zoop

zoopa zoop zoop-a

zoopa zoop zoop

Zoopa zoop zoop-a

Zoopa zoop zoop

Bazoopa zoop zoop-a

zoopa zoop zoop

Zoop-aaaaa

zoopa zoopa zoopa zoop zoop!

Some people now believe that this song is a Moss-Skweeto cautionary tale about the consequences of indifference, but we really don't know if this is true, since we never bothered to ask.

    Over the summer, late every Thursday evening, Darryl sat on a folding chair behind a shaky little table on a cramped little landing, between two flights of stairs. It was a choke point for the entrance of the upstairs dance floor, where Havanna '59 held Salsa night. It was somewhat sad to see Darryl sit there on his rickety little chair behind his wobbly little table. He looked timid. But in another way, he was empowered and emboldened: you either paid Darryl to dance upstairs, or you didn't dance up upstairs. Some people always tried to wrangle their way through for free, but Darryl never let those cheapskates pass. Mostly, people paid him. Some were people who just loved to dance, some were old white men looking for a one night stand with a young senorita or a pretty young black lady, and some were young senoritas and pretty young black ladies interested in alluring old white men into buying them drinks. The old white men were always glad to oblige the young ladies with tasty and potent cocktails, that is, until the old farts realized that there was zero chance of romance in their near future, at which point, the well dried up.

    On the hottest, steamiest nights, the boss lady would open all the windows and roll-up doors, and transform the bar into an open-air environment. She claimed this created an atmosphere reminiscent of Havanna in 1959, though she couldn't possibly know this, since she was born in Kankakee in 1965. Plus, she said, it made Salsa night all the more steamy and seductive. What the boss lady wouldn't say was that she was just too cheap to turn on the air conditioning. But, she did turn on the ceiling fans, though mistakenly in reverse direction. This created a draft from the downstairs bar, up the stairwell past Darryl, and beyond to the second floor dancehall. Darryl, being an astrophysicist, understood that when this air rushed up the stairs, he was sitting dead center inside a venturi: a wind tunnel. You would think this would be nice, having a steady breeze in the middle of a stagnant, humid summer night, but you would be wrong. The local Moss-Skweetos were often drawn to Havanna '59 by the sweaty summer stench of writhing salsa dancers. As the bugs congregated in the air just outside the front of the bar, they found themselves sucked into the downstairs windows, carried up the stairs, and forced through the venturi. The bugs desperately grabbed onto whatever they could, to avoid being sucked up further to who knew where. But the best place to grab, was not the slick walls, nor the tile floors, nor even the cigar-smoke stained ceiling. The best thing to grab onto was at the narrowest part of the venturi, the choke point: Darryl. While the people upstairs shook the floors in a relatively bug free, drunk, hip-grinding ecstasy, Darryl swatted and swatted the bugs in the air around him, on his neck, and on his arms. He suffered incessant bites, torment, and torture by the unrelenting little irritants sent his way by his cheapskate boss.

    Darryl returned home from every Salsa night itchy and scratching. He'd take an antihistamine pill, lather himself with calamine lotion, and update his resume.

Millinia ago on the Moss-Skweeto home world, space mission control specialists watched as the wormhole closed on the star cruiser, slicing off the backside of the ship, where the brakes were located. Mission control specialists quickly realized this wasn't good. They immediately scrambled an emergency search and rescue team, but soon realized that they couldn't deploy the team, since the star cruiser itself opened the wormhole, and since no one on the home world had bothered to ask where they were going. Embarrassed and ashamed by this oversight, the Moss-Skweetos lowered their collective heads and kicked the proverbial dirt. Their only recourse was to wait for the star cruiser to contact mission control to let them know where they had gone.

When the Moss-Skweetos' crippled basketball shaped ship hurtled toward the surface of the Earth, at least one clear-thinking crew member managed to send a mayday distress call back to the home world. But, since they had travelled billions of light-years across the universe to Earth, it would take billions of light-years for their message to reach home, and billions of light-years for a rescue party to come and get them. The bugs soon understood that if they could open another wormhole, they could send another distress call through it, and reach the home world within minutes. But since their star cruiser and all of its advanced technology now lay destroyed under water, and under a ginormous bed of sand and slimy

Earth silt, they had no hardware to open another wormhole. It just wasn't going to happen. In the meantime, the bugs would just have to figure out how to cope and survive on this new world until they could figure out another way to call home. So they did.

It turns out that Chincoteague, and its neighboring island Assateague, shared many traits with the Moss-Skweeto home world landscape: namely, it was often hot, with low lying marshes and many, many stagnant pools of water. So it wasn't hard to make themselves at home.

Food soon became an issue and they made do with whatever they could find. At first, they sucked the blood of our oversized salamander-like ancestors, then dinosaurs, then mammals, and they survived on these things until one species eventually dominated the planet and therefore dominated the Moss-Skweeto diet: monkeys.

The bugs watched as monkeys got smarter and smarter, to the point where they came up for a word for themselves: humans. Having a word for themselves gave them inspiration to create other words for other things, which in turn helped them spur invention and technology. As technology progressed, the Moss-Skweetos tried to help move things along a little quicker so they could call home a little sooner. They tried to communicate, to give them prompts and advice, but they weren't very successful. Humans proved incapable or unimaginative. Human's could have developed cell phones, and cars and airplanes and spaceships and Burger Chefs much sooner than they did, but for the fact that they simply never paid attention to the prompts nor the advice.

This frustrated the bugs to no end. They swarmed the heads of the humans in frantic attempts to gain their attention, so the humans could help the bugs. But this backfired. They had fed off of the blood of humans for so long that humans saw them as nothing more than vicious irritants. So the bugs were just swatted, and smushed leaving many Moss-Skweetos to feel this tactic was shortsighted at best. The bugs also made the mistake of not foreseeing that though the humans were still pretty stupid, they eventually would become smart enough to invent bug spray, which would prove lethal and even genocidal.

Though the bugs were without their own superior technology, they tried to communicate and influence humans via one talent that all Moss-Skweetos are born with: the ability to generate, carry, and administer viruses. Sometimes, a viral infection succeeded, but more often the humans just got sick.

In the meantime, the bugs had to wait for the human technology to catch up. After an interminable time, the human mind eventually grew big enough and smart enough to create and install a high tech scientific installation on the Delmarva that the bugs could use for their own ends: the word they gave this installation was Wallops.

It was named after John Wallop, a white guy who was given a sizable chunk of land by King William III of England, who apparently was happy to give away land that he had neither seen, nor actually owned. Two hundred years later, the Commonwealth of Virginia seized the land because neither John Wallop, nor his descendants, had paid any taxes on this land, given to him by someone who didn't even own it.

Another hundred years later, the humans and their government built an installation on that seized land, so people could look up at the sky, and into space. They even had a word for this activity: science. Humans were so proud of their new scientific facility that they then named it after a tax delinquent. Over the years they expanded the capacity of the science they could do there, by adding to what they already had there. They paved a few criss-crossing runways so they could fly airplanes for atmospheric investigation, and then, they even made large pointy tubes that they shot up into space for various reasons. They installed a dozen or so parabolic telescopes, for looking and listening deeper into space, and for sending their voices there too.

When the humans made these telescopes the bugs were ecstatic. The bugs, being a superior race, understood how to co-opt this technology to call home. So every now and again, the bugs congregated and completely blanketed the parabolic dish to try to hack into it. They joined legs, proboscises and abdomens with each other, forming a net of bugs encompassing the body of the parabolic dish. They'd then flap their wings, vibrate their abdomens and thoraxes, searching for the right sympathetic harmonic resonance to overtake the telescope. This resonance could open a wormhole and send a distress call through it. But, this became a terribly risky endeavor that ultimately cost the lives of billions of bugs.

In old science fiction movies, humans tend to have only one statement prepared for any encounter with an alien race: "take me to your leader." The alien race usually complies happily, and that's when all of the trouble starts. But humans who have constantly been in close proximity with the Moss-Skweetos for thousands of years never seemed to think that the statement, "take me to your leader" bore any relevance in this circumstance. Come to think of it, the bugs never thought to say this to the humans either, but that's probably because throughout their history, they never made science fiction movies, nor did they watch the ones made by the humans.

    To complicate matters further, humans usually don't want to hear the answers to the questions they, themselves ask. Think about the last time you were at a party, and a stranger, toting a nearly empty tumbler of scotch, approached you. Cursory introductions were exchanged and the stranger then asked what you did for a living. You responded that you were an astronaut who just risked your life every day over the span of two years living in a tin foil space-can orbiting the Earth at 17,000 miles per hour. There, you performed research that was crucial for the survival of humankind. But before you can finish your sentence you noticed a glaze forming on the stranger's eyeballs, and you also saw that his attention had turned inward in an effort to formulate a thought, and then a sentence, and then another sentence, for a response. He interrupted your answer to the question he asked, and for the next half an hour he told you all about his exciting career at Burger Chef.

    We've been told that humans are innately curious creatures, but I'm not so sure. I'm convinced that if we find a captive audience, we'd rather enhance our miserable existence, not so much to convince our audience that our life is good, but rather, to convince ourselves. We talk a lot, we humans, and because we do, we rarely listen.

Since humans, with our proverbial tumbler of scotch, were never particularly interested in understanding the Moss-Skweetos, we never found out where the bugs were from, or what they did, or how smart they were. We never said "take me to your leader" so we never learned if the bugs followed some fellow who guided the direction of their society through principles and laws. Nor did we find out if they instead operated collectively, like a lot of Earth's bugs; hives crawling with individuals whose duties are driven by some base instinct. Duties that when combined with the individual duties of the next guy, and the next guy after that, and so on, form a society that responds like a single organism with its own actions, thoughts and motivations. Sadly, to this day, we still don't know much about the makeup of the Moss-Skweetos' society, and we certainly never received any technological advancements from them, because no one ever cared to listen. But the Scotch was good.

  Molly was now making adequate money from tips, but she still desperately wanted more from life, and she always wanted to be somewhere other than where she currently was. She still powdered and painted up her face and dyed her hair black-hole-black, but she also somehow took on a more respectable demeanor for the patrons at Don's Seafood Restaurant. She longed to be a rebel, and she quietly resented herself every time she approached a customer's table with a welcoming smile, and welcoming words. She called the old men "luv," and the old ladies, "sweetheart," not because she meant it, but because she desired a bigger tip: it usually worked. She smiled so much, that by mid-shift, her whole face was sore. Molly didn't like serving food to people, and she really hated collecting their dirty dishes, but she learned to suppress her baser revulsions, to act professionally, and as a result, she became quite good at her job.

  But every time Molly returned to her waitress station, her smile faded. She oversaw the dining room like a bored day care operator, looking for signs that her charges needed something: a refill, dessert, the check. She regarded the diners with considerable disdain. It was utterly dreadful for her to stand alone in the corner, while watching a bunch of other people eat expensive food and have all the fun. So, Molly often leaned against the wall at the waitress station yearning to be somewhere else: anywhere else.

When not at work, Molly spent her free time at home browsing through magazines she had stolen from beauty salons or any other place that had them lying around. When she came across a picture of an exotic place she'd like to visit, Molly cut it out, took it to work and taped it on the wall of the waitress station. Neither the other waitresses nor the managers seemed to mind. The pictures helped Molly forget her annoying clients. She could instead lose herself within some stolen image; driving across the triple arches at Glacier National Park, climbing Les Eclaireurs Lighthouse in Ushuaia, soaking up the sun on some whitewashed terrace in Santorini, mingling with puffins on the Faroe Islands.

One night at the end of her shift, Molly left work and plodded across Don's parking lot toward the docks where she had parked her two hundred dollar K car. A glimmer from the water caught her eye. She paused to look. A gentle wind pushed riffles across the Queen Sound Channel setting the entire waterway ablaze with moonlight. She thought about the moon and wondered what it would be like to walk on its surface, "Who am I kidding?" She sneered. "I can't even swing a weekend in Byoona Vista."

Darryl was smart enough to calculate the trajectory of a loaf of bread launched from Earth to within a few feet of a ten mile long asteroid orbiting the farthest reach of our solar system, but he was still unable to fathom why he couldn't find a job better than the doorman at Salsa night. Sitting on his wobbly little chair behind his wobbly little table in the bug infested venturi, he had plenty of time to ponder as he wrapped blue Tyvek wristbands on pretty young senoritas, young black ladies, and lecherous old white men. He thought, "if I can't get a job outside the academic world, why not try inside the academic world?"

Darryl carefully retyped his resume using computer templates and nice fonts. He gracefully adorned the document with intelligent enhancements and ornamental flourishes to gild his experience for a potential reader. Humans have a word for this: lying. He slid the resume into a manila envelope along with a copy of his dissertation, *The probable existence of intelligent and evolved life on other planets, and the improbability of Earthly inhabitants to ever get actual proof of Extra Terrestrial existence.* He then mailed the envelope to the National Aeronautics and Space Administration: NASA for short.

As Darryl wrapped a band around a young lady's wrist, he thought, "NASA, it's academic." Now as you already know, words mean stuff, and "it's academic" often refers to a situation where smart people argue about outlandish ideas and theories, with no real intention to do anything about these ideas and theories. There certainly is an academic aspect to the interaction between scientists and mathematicians and theoretical physicists and what not, so Darryl was partially right when he supposed that NASA was an academic entity. But, NASA also had engineers and astronauts who were keenly interested in putting theory into practice. That is, they intended to make, and do, real stuff with their outlandish ideas. "It's academic" applied to NASA, even though it didn't.

NASA officials read Darryl's dissertation and were impressed with his ideas and his lexicon, plus his breadth of theoretical knowledge. His academic arguments raised some interested eyebrows from some very smart people at NASA; people who wanted to hear more about Darryl's ideas, and then see Darryl implement them, the latter of which Darryl had never anticipated.

So NASA offered Darryl a job at the government airport facility named after the tax cheat, John Wallop, across from Chincoteague on the Delmarva. A place where very smart people think about space, peer into space, and then shoot large pointy tubes, rockets, into space: a place that is both academic and practical. They gave him an office, an old government issued metal desk, an outdated computer, a stapler, and a plastic phone. The wobbly chair and table at Havanna '59 were history, and now he had an actual office with accoutrements, leading Darryl to believe that he had finally arrived.

Darryl's new NASA boss escorted him down the hall, through an old hangar, past a dusty old twin engine Beech 18 airplane. He opened a crusty old door and led Darryl outside to the aviation ramp where they stopped and admired a massive white parabolic radio telescope. "You'll be using this," the boss said, "to look up there," he pointed to the sky, "for actual proof of Extra Terrestrial life."

Suddenly, it all became very real for Darryl. This new job wasn't academic as he understood the word to mean. Having a desk and a phone and a stapler weren't the end game. He was expected to produce actual results. NASA wanted him to find real aliens: intelligent life that originated from someplace other than Earth.

He then felt a twinge on his forearm. Nestled among the hairs he found a slender, long-legged bug piercing his skin, drawing his blood. "Ow!" Darryl said under his breath. He smacked the Moss-Skweeto, smushing him and smearing coagulant gore down his arm.

"If intelligent life is out there," he assured his boss, "I'll find it."

For a long while, most of human history, a really long while actually, the only way to get to Chincoteague from the Delmarva was to swim across Queen Sound Channel. Humans stood on the shore and looked over at the island and even though they weren't smart enough to build a boat yet, they were however, smart enough to question whether the swim across all of that water, just to come ashore on an island full of bugs, was worth all the effort. When humans did become smart enough to build boats, the trip became doable, but it would take days to paddle over to Chincoteague, battle with the bugs, do whatever else they did over there at that time, and then paddle back. At that same time, humans were still smart enough to question whether it was worth all the effort. Over the centuries, humans developed better boats to make boating easier. They added masts and sails so the wind would do all the work, but after a while even that seemed slow and tedious, and again they questioned whether it was worth all the effort. It wasn't until recent human history that someone thought to mount a motor on the stern of a boat. Humans found the trip to Chincoteague fast, and relatively easy, at least for a little while. But when the automobile finally appeared on the Delmarva, people became extraordinarily lazy. They didn't want to have to get out of their car, in order to hop into a boat, flounder about across the channel to the island, where they then would have to walk around. They wanted a boat to take them and their car over to Chincoteague, so they could drive around the small island. So, some smart human developed a ferry system that would accommodate them and their newly acquired lax lifestyle. The problem was, there were no real roads on Chincoteague, so the ferry had to first take paving equipment over so car owners would have somewhere to drive once they got there. It didn't matter that all of this was a huge effort to make the trip effortless for people and their cars. But, people didn't care about any of that, because they weren't smart enough to realize any of that, and eventually, people came to think that even the ferry was slow and tedious, and therefore folks wondered if the ferry was worth all the effort.

By 1919, John B. Whealton, a resident of Chincoteague, had been around long enough to see some of the evolution of travel between the Delmarva and the island. He had also been around long enough to hear all the different people whine and complain about the tedium of making the trip by boat, in all of its various forms. And many, many times he heard people ask if it was worth all the effort.

Whealton, who owned a business on the island, needed it to be worth all the effort if he wanted tourists to visit and spend their money, so he could stay in business. And although, over the years, travel to the island got easier and easier, people still found something to complain about. That's just human nature: they aren't happy unless they're complaining. So, Whealton thought and thought until he figured out a way to make it really easy for people to get to the island. What he needed was an idea so easy and convenient that they couldn't quickly find a way to complain about it. That idea was a causeway: a raised road traversing Queen Sound Channel, linking Chincoteague to the Delmarva. Boats and ferries would be rendered obsolete, because people could drive their own cars back and forth to the island, whenever they wanted, in a fraction of the time. John took his proposal to the state legislature, arguing that this added convenience would be good for the island and its businesses, and therefore, its residents and their wallets. The legislature, considering potential tax revenue, and ignoring potential tax cheats like John Wallops, agreed and opened the project to construction bids.

    Whealton then coincidentally formed the Chincoteague Toll Road and Bridge Company. He offered to do the job for $144,000, a humongous sum in 1919, but also coincidentally, a small enough amount to undercut all of the other bidders. Whealton won the lucrative government contract, and then dumped load after load of rip rap into the water, until it formed a narrow ribbon leading to the island. He then built a road on top of that narrow ribbon of rocks, and for the first time since the Moss-Skweeto star cruiser severed the isthmus, Whealton had reconnected Chincoteague Island with the Delmarva.

    Construction was complete when a small arched bridge connected the end of the causeway to the island. Four thousand people then attended a grand opening ceremony on Chincoteague. Ninety six cars drove across the brand new road to get there. Many state VIPs were there, including the governor. Millions of curious or hungry Moss-Skweetos attended, forcing all of the human attendees to cover up, incessantly swat the air around them, and hurry through the event. A ceremonial ribbon was hastily cut, and as if on cue, it started to rain: hard. The causeway became inundated with water, and flooded so badly that all ninety six cars were stranded on Chincoteague. The boats and barges and ferries made obsolete by the causeway were once again called into service to rescue people stuck on the island, and to take their cars back to the Delmarva.

John Whealton, embarrassed, but not defeated, simply dumped more rip rap on the causeway to raise his road high enough to make it usable again, even in a hard rain. People soon forgot about the fiasco as Whealton's causeway made life a little faster, and a little easier. And since they couldn't find much to complain about, the road then transformed in their minds from a novelty convenience, to a necessity. That's when John Whealton drove a truck loaded with construction materials to the entrance of the causeway, and built a toll booth.

At first the residents revolted, but soon conceded. No one would admit it out loud, but no one was the least bit interested in once again using boats to make the trip across the water. So, everyone just groused under his or her breath and forked over the toll. Tourists on the other hand, especially cheapskate tourists, who had no actual need to get to Chincoteague, other than a vacation, which is not a need, found it easy to forego the toll, turn around and drive somewhere else for the weekend. A decade later, the vast majority of people giving John Whealton money to cross the causeway were the people of Chincoteague, and they were long since tired of lining Whealton's pockets with coin. They demanded that he remove the toll, which he reluctantly did.

After that, the drive across the causeway became absolutely pleasant. There were no tolls, only beautiful, unobstructed views of the marshes, sparkling sunlit waterways, and tidal landscapes.

Tourists even started regularly driving over to the island, where they spent their money and contributed to the local economy.

Whealton, again, had been embarrassed, but not defeated. One day, he, along with his new business partner, Elian James, floated a barge full of construction materials out to the entrance of the causeway. They pile-drove some large pillars into the marsh by the road, built a rectangular frame on them, nailed up some plywood and glued large swaths of paper to it. It was a billboard, an advertisement actually, for the Chincoteague Inn. And not too long after the billboard was erected, Whealton and James caught wind that the inn kept filling up with tourists while the other hotels languished. So they built another billboard after the first one, also right next to the causeway, to promote whoever wanted to pay to be promoted. And when that one worked, they built another, and another, and another, until billboards lined the entire causeway like rectangular ducks in a row.

But residents and tourists of Chincoteague didn't much mind the billboards. It didn't much matter to them that an immense natural beauty was hidden behind a bunch of garish advertisements. People tended not to notice the billboards in the same way they rarely noticed the bugs, because they were always there: like they had always been there. For younger generations who drove the causeway, the signs had actually always been there, even before they were born. The pleasant view never existed to them, so how could they miss something they never had? In any case, people were always in too much of a hurry to get to the island or to the Delmarva. They were in too much of a rush to take in the world around them. They preferred to just get there, wherever there was. A nice view just didn't matter to anyone anymore, as long as getting there was easy.

But what really made residents and tourists complacent and kept them from asking if it was worth all the effort, was that the advertisements made travel along the causeway free: except, that it didn't. Tourists and residents who believed the billboards were just mildly interesting signs sticking up out of the water, would have, if they paid attention, later found themselves handing over large wads of money to the very hotels and restaurants whose names adorned the advertisements. So, not only was the causeway not free to drive on, it actually cost people more money than just handing over a few nickels to a guy in a toll booth. Though humans are still smart enough to realize that it's too much trouble to swim to Chincoteague, they still aren't smart enough to realize when they've been had by the likes of John Whealton.

In the end, the causeway, and especially its billboards, made John Whealton a rich man. He retired with a hefty annuity, selling his share of the business to Elian James, who passed the business down to his son, John James. To this day, John still floats a flat bottom boat out to the channel, fighting clouds of bugs, in order to glue large messages to the signs. People receive a subliminal nudge to spend money, among other things, while believing that the causeway is free to use, and worth all the effort.

When tip dried up, money was tight for Molly, and when it was especially tight she'd stop by the Burger Chef on her way to work. She'd walk in the side door and approach the counter knowing that her father worked the cash register near the end of the breakfast shift, and as usual, he would see her walk in.

"The usual ma'am?" Dad grinned.

"Like you don't know," Molly smirked.

"Coming right up." He turned to the food service rack.

Molly leaned against the counter, trying to look cool, but in doing so, belied a nervous undertone to Burger Chef employees who knew Molly was there for a handout.

Dad snapped open a paper bag and placed a breakfast biscuit and hash browns carefully inside. He strode to the soda fountain where an employee handed him a drink already filled for Molly's "usual."

Molly forced a smile at the employee, though she couldn't hide her embarrassment.

Dad passed the bag and the drink across the counter to Molly. "Here you go, Boo." He was the only person to call her that, and she hated it, except that she didn't.

Never once did she ask Dad not to call her that name, even though it was also a painful reminder of the phrase, "What about Boo?"

Molly was six years old:

Mom shrieked at Dad. He didn't have time for an argument. He was a walking polyester hamburger rushing to get ready for work. Mom, as usual, was unemployed and unemployable. She smoked until her pores exuded nicotine. She reeked of cheap perfume from the dollar store. No one knew her real hair color. She didn't care.

"What do you mean?" Dad shouted at Mom.

"I don't know." Mom shrugged, acting coy.

Molly kneeled in front of the TV, immersed herself in Sesame Street, and pretended not to notice yet another fight between Mom and Dad. Mom lived life sullen and distracted. Dad often tried to find out what was wrong. Mom would never answer, preferring instead to silently pout. Dad would console her, and placate her, until she blew up at him, and he responded in-kind.

"How can you not know?"

"I just don't! Okay?"

"It's not okay! What do you mean?"

Mom hesitated, and her hands quavered as she spoke, "It's just not working out."

"Yeah, I know, it's tough, but what part of this isn't working out?"

"I gotta go." Mom said and dashed to the front door.

"Where?"

"Anywhere," she paused. "but where I am."

"You can't go!" Dad yelled. "I have to go to work!" He pointed at Molly, "What about Boo?"

Molly mustered the courage to glance over her shoulder at Mom, who could barely make eye contact with her own daughter.

"Bye." She said, and walked out, never to be seen again.

Dad started to run out after Mom, but he stopped himself. He instead knelt beside Molly and hugged her. "It's okay, Boo," he said. "I'll call in sick. I'm not going anywhere."

Dad rang up Molly's meal, pulled out his wallet and placed the money into the register. Molly was quitely grateful by this small gesture. Though she hated him so much during her teenage years, as an adult, she gradually began to comprehend who he was; a sad little man, held back in life by his own choices. But he was also someone willing to spend five bucks to feed his daughter, even though he probably had only six bucks in his wallet. He wasn't going anywhere in his career, nor was he going anywhere where he couldn't help Molly.

"Thanks," she smiled.

"Of course, Boo."

Molly exited across the dining room. She understood that she wasn't going anywhere either because her own choices held her back. She wished she could change that, but she was a lot like her Dad in some respects. She knew this now. They had been close for such a long time.

But, she never had the chance to grow up around her Mom and learn who she was as a person. She didn't know how sullen her Mom could be, how she could endlessly sulk, or how flighty she could be. How she always wanted to be on the move, to go places, to be a bon vivant without consequence.

Molly knew none of this, because she never knew her Mom. And not knowing her Mom meant that in many ways she didn't know herself.

Darryl analyzed a squiggly line that appeared on his computer screen. He hadn't seen anything like it before. At first he thought it was a waveform: sound. But he discounted that because it wasn't a normal waveform. It was different. Not right. It didn't make sense. He checked the software settings, and they looked okay, so he relaunched the program. The squiggly line popped up again on his computer screen and he reexamined it.

"Huh," Darryl grunted.

For the next few hours Darryl studied the persistent line, believing that some anomaly had corrupted the waveform, or even his computer's software. No matter what he did, or where he clicked, the same unintelligible squiggly line popped up on his screen, over and over, until he couldn't take it any more.

"Corrupt code," Darryl surmised. "I'll fix it later." He shut down his computer to let it rest, and went to lunch.

Darryl fed a few dollars into the vending machine in the NASA employee break room. He pushed the "C" button and then the "3" button. Clever mechanisms inside the machine retrieved and dropped a prepackaged chicken salad sandwich to a basin within the bottom of the machine. Darryl leaned over and pushed open a swinging door to get his sandwich. He sat at a formica table in the middle of the room and peeled back a plastic film, unsealing the sandwich container. One bite revealed a cold, bland, moderately soggy, and mostly dissatisfying sandwich, at best. He laid the uneaten portion across the top of its container and washed down a mouthful of mush with a swig of soda.

Across the break room, Darryl noticed that as he wretched on the sandwich, he was being watched by a coworker. He was the only other guy there, and Darryl wondered why he had not noticed him before. Darryl set his soda down and acknowledged the man, who then said, "Pretty bad, isn't it?"

"Yeah," Darryl agreed, "pretty bad."

"You'd think a bunch of smart guys at NASA would be smart enough to have a good cafeteria on site," said the man.

"You'd think." Darryl agreed.

"But they aren't," the man chuckled.

"They aren't," Darryl agreed, before forcing another bite.

"I'm Dave."

"Darryl."

"I know. I work across the hall from you."

"Oh, you…" Darryl wondered how he could not have noticed this.

"Most of the guys that work here go over to the island for lunch."

"Yeah?" Darryl asked, "is it far?"

"No," said Dave, "it's just a short drive over the causeway." He then added, "it's worth all the effort."

Darryl looked at his pathetic sandwich and thought, "what the heck?" He got up and tossed what was left into the closest trash can. "I'm convinced." He nodded at Dave, walked to the door but paused, "got any recommendations?"

"Don's Seafood Restaurant is good."

"Yeah?"

"Yeah," Dave assured him.

"Have you tried it?"

Dave shook his head, "Oh, no. No," he said. "No."

"Oh," Darryl nodded, unsure what to think. "Well, I'll give it a try." He then noticed that Dave was himself halfway finished eating a prepackaged chicken salad sandwich from the machine, and he felt a little sorry for him. "Would you like to go with me?" Darryl asked.

"Yeah," Dave replied, "No, no," he chuckled nervously, "too many bugs" and then he added, "and people," and then he added to that, "not sure which are worse."

Darryl drove across the causeway. He barely paid attention to the string of billboards sticking out of the marsh. He fixated instead on how to find Don's Seafood Restaurant once he got to the island. He would find that it wasn't hard at all to locate, because the island isn't that big, and Don's is pretty much right there where you drive onto the island. Darryl parked next to a two hundred dollar Plymouth K car in the rear lot next to the Waterfront Park and the docks. He went around front and entered through the main entrance. The hostess saw Darryl, grabbed a menu and utensils wrapped in a paper napkin, and approached him.

"One for lunch?" she asked. He nodded and she led him to the upstairs dining room next to the bar. She stopped at a table by a large bank of windows overlooking the Queen Sound Channel and the causeway he just drove in on.

"How's this?" She asked.

"Good." He said, sitting down and scooting the chair up to the table.

"Your server will be right with you."

"Thanks," Darryl said, fidgeting in his seat.

The hostess walked across the room and swung by the waitress station signaling to some unseen person that a customer had just been seated.

A young woman emerged, turning the corner of the station. A smile eased onto her face as her lanky frame glided over to Darryl's table. Her face was powder white, her lips, blood red, her eyes, cerulean. She had tattoo sleeves and a spiderweb plumage on her egret neck. Her hair was so unnaturally black that, well, you know the rest. For Darryl, there was only one word to describe her: exotic.

The waitress sidled up to his table. "Mornin' luv," she said.

Though Darryl knew it was technically afternoon, and thought he never had a tendency to drop the letter "g" at the end of any word when he talked, he was currently unable to reply any way except by saying, "mornin'."

"I'm Molly, I'll be your server today." Her smile grew a little bigger, "What'll you be drinking today, luv?"

Darryl stuttered, fumbled with the menu for a moment, and unable to quickly find where the drinks were listed, he blurted out a drink order, though he wasn't exactly sure what he had just asked for.

"Half/half iced tea," Molly replied, scribbling on her waiter's pad. "Alright. I'll be back right away to take your order."

He gaped at her as she walked back to the waitress station. Darryl, who had an intellect capable of understanding and articulating the impossible realities of quantum entanglement, at that moment, couldn't fathom his desire for Molly, he couldn't connect this newfound infatuation with the very probable reality that Don's Seafood Restaurant was about to become his new lunch hangout.

Chincoteague's official bird is the mosquito. You heard me right: mosquito. Why all of a sudden, in this story, you ask, would I use this word? Because, it's the word we've grown accustomed to in real life. Therefore, it actually is the right word to use, except for the fact that it isn't. About now you're wondering why it could or could not be the right word, since it is the official word we've been using for so long outside of this story. I suppose that makes you an amateur etymologist. And, if it is the official word, why have we been hearing that other word so much throughout this story? Why, I ask in response, would a bug be made an official bird? Because it seems, that sometimes, words don't mean stuff.

During the first quarter of the nineteenth century, it was fashionable for gentlemen scientists to board creaky old ships and sail to far-away lands to study indigenous flora and fauna. During the first quarter of the nineteenth century, many gentleman scientists still considered Chincoteauge Island a far-away land. Dr. Richard Mills was one of them. He was a dashing young English gentleman on a personal quest to venture up the right hand coast of America in search of exotic places. He'd stop at various villages along the way, where he billed himself a naturalist to any villager willing to listen. Every time he wandered into a new place, he asked the villagers to direct him to the best local area where he could find undisturbed nature to observe for his scientific endeavors. Thinking he was just some idle rich guy in search of a purpose, the villagers were happy to point him in just about any direction away from the village, especially if that meant that they wouldn't have to listen to him go on any longer about "exploring far-away lands," which to them meant, "the back yard." The villagers it seemed, just wanted to get back to their daily chores, since daily chores, unlike scientific endeavors, kept villagers from dying by starvation. Usually with a grateful tip of his hat, Dr. Mills was off to the woods, observing plants and animals, collecting specimens, taking notes and drawing elaborate sketches in his gentlemanly, leather-bound notebook. One day, sitting on a log watching beetles eat through solid wood and then poop it out as sawdust, Dr. Mills observed that his book contained far more notes and drawings pertaining to bugs than anything else. "Curious," he thought.

At that very moment he might have concluded that he was not simply a naturalist, but more specifically, he was an entomologist. But that word did not yet exist on Earth. That's because in order for words to mean stuff, stuff usually has to provide a reason to make up a word for stuff in the first place. So therefore, at that point, there was no way Dr. Richard Mills could have been an entomologist. That is, unless he decided that there was a reason that studying bugs should be a subset of being a naturalist. He could then decide to refer back in time to his university days when he studied the ancient Greek language. He could recollect appropriate synonyms like entomon, which means "insect," and logia which means"to study." Dr. Mills could then combine the words on the spot to create a new word, entomology. If he had done so, sitting on that log in the woods somewhere outside of some village, he would have been the world's first entomologist. But he didn't. So he didn't become an entomologist, nor it seems, an etymologist.

Now fascinated by insects, Dr. Mills worked his way up the right hand side of the American coast. He asked villager after villager where he could find the best concentration of bugs to study. The farther north he got, the more people pointed him towards Chincoteague. So he went there. When he arrived and first stepped ashore on the island, he was immediately delighted to discover that the concentration of bugs was far more dense than even the best reports he had previously received. He then felt a bite on his neck, then his cheek, and then his forehead, and like so many people before him, and after him, he became immediately distraught that the concentration of bugs was far more dense than even the best reports he previously received. He flailed his arms frantically at the cloud of bugs orbiting his head, and he repeatedly slapped and squashed droves of bugs attacking his flesh. He hastily flung his scientific gear over his shoulder and made a mad dash for cover, any cover, which turned out to be a rickety, weather-beaten shanty by the water's edge.

He pounded on the door but didn't wait for a response, rudely thrusting himself inside. Bugs floated in the air, and rested on the walls, though fewer than outside. They too rudely let themselves into the shanty through sliver sized cracks between the clapboards. A scraggly old man sat on a milk stool in the middle of the room. At his knees, a cast iron pot steamed over a dying fire while the old man dissected and ate a reddish, faceless, cooked crab. His hair was long and matted, his clothes were filthy, and mud was caked over every inch of his exposed skin. He appeared unbothered that a stranger just barged into his house, like it was a normal occurrence on the island.

"I beg your pardon," Dr. Mills removed his hat.

"Leave it on." said the man without even looking. Dr. Mills was taken aback because the scroungy old fart actually spoke with the clarity and articulation of a gentleman.

"I beg your…"

The man pointed at Dr. Mill's hat. "You'll want to leave that on," he said, and then added, "protection."

"Oh," Dr. Mills set the hat back on his head and then he started to explain himself. "I'm sorry to barge in like that, old chap, but if I didn't, I think the bugs would have eaten me whole, bones and all."

"Uh huh," the man grunted while tugging crab meat from a claw with his teeth.

Dr. Mills, was at a loss. "Umm…pardon my ill manners, I'm Dr. Richard Mills," he touched the brim of his hat but remembered the old man's advice and did not tip it.

The man discarded the empty claw, picked up the crab's body and abruptly cracked its underbelly open, "James," he answered, scraping the devil out with a mud caked forefinger.

"Well James…"

"Mr. James," he interrupted.

"I beg your pardon?"

"Mr. James." He then shrugged, "Who cares? Call me Elijah." He set the crab down on a filthy tin plate and asked, "What are you doing here Dr. Mills?"

"Again, there was a dreadful horde of bugs outside..."

"I mean on the island." Elijah interrupted.

"Oh," Dr. Mills absentmindedly brushed bugs off the breast of his frock coat, "I'm a naturalist, come to study bugs."

Elijah James set his plate on his lap, and for the first time became very interested in Dr. Mills, "The mosquitoes?" he asked.

You heard him right.

Elijah James was the town lunatic. He was dirty and smelly and often walked through the streets ranting strange ideas, using strange words. One word that he repeated over and over, the word that everyone grew exhausted of hearing from his mouth over the years, the word that estranged him from all of the sane people on the island, was the word "mosquito."

But Elijah wasn't always the town lunatic. Like Dr. Richard Mills, he was once a gentleman in search of adventure. He was also in search of a fortune. Stepping from a ship onto a wharf in Virginia's capital city, his attention was almost immediately drawn to a bill posted on a wall. In big letters, it read, "Free Land Grant." Intrigued, Elijah James stepped forward and leaned in to read the fine print. "Parcels for the taking," it read. "One only has to take."

A barrel chested man noticed Elijah's interest in the flyer and sidled up to him, "The ship leaves in the morning," he winked, and smiled. Elijah smiled too and in the morning found himself on a ship bound for Chincoteague Island. He stood at the gunwale, green and seasick from the choppy waters of the bay. But this he could endure, since he was fast becoming a gentleman land owner, witnessing the genesis of his empire of property and wealth.

But as Dr. Mills stood there, he didn't recognize the gentleman within Elijah. Instead he faced a filthy, muddy, crusty old man with crab remnants stuck in his beard. Elijah had been forced into this condition by his own decision to ignore the fine print of his land grant, which he never bothered to read. Had he read it, Elijah would have discovered what all land grantees eventually discovered: the terms of a grant required a person to settle on a piece of land for a period of several years before they owned that property free and clear, and before they could sell that property for any money. If they left the land, they forfeited everything. And like Elijah, most settlers found that their promised land was just a miserable swath of Earth, and they soon understood why someone else, who probably didn't even own the land, was giving it away. The hardships of just existing on a land grant proved too unbearable for most people, forcing many to give up, to abandon their dreams, to just get the hell out, and go back to an easier city life of decent coffee and regular meals. By the time Dr. Mills barged into the shanty, Elijah James was 9 years in to what he called his "ten year sentence" on a postage stamp of bug infested marsh-land that flooded every time the sky drizzled.

An early resident of Chincoteague, Elijah James was also the Moss-Skweetos first moderately successful attempt to communicate with humans. Commando bugs bit Elijah and infected him with a mind control virus. They designed the virus to travel to Elijah's brain with a message of first contact between species. The message was, "We are the Moss-Skweetos from Galaxy ACR1964. We need your help to return home. Please stop swatting us." The bugs hoped that Elijah would receive the message and then relay it to other humans, who in turn would hopefully find compassion in their hearts to help the Moss-Skweetos. So, the bugs attacked Elijah incessantly until they successfully infected him with their viral message. But Elijah James' peculiar DNA proved somewhat resistant to the virus, and only served to corrupt the bugs' message. As a result, Elijah James feverishly stumbled across the island confronting other townsfolk with bizarre assertions of mind controlling aliens, which seemed especially deranged to people who lived long before the advent of Earth's space age. Elijah spoke in fragments, incomplete messages that he insisted were placed in his head by some cosmic force. He accosted people in the street, repeating one word over and over again. It was a word, that wasn't even a word at the time: "mosquito." The townsfolk didn't know what this word meant, because to them, it wasn't a word. And if it wasn't a word, how could it mean anything?

The bugs infected Elijah James many times with many messages, but their attempts to contact humans through him never ended well, and no coherent message was ever delivered. Elijah's mad man appearance combined with his frequent rants throughout the town had only succeeded in turning him into a pariah. So, he spent most of his time alone in his shanty, eating reddish, faceless crabs while serving out his ten year sentence, all for a spongy, waterlogged slab of dirt.

Dr. Mills spent the next several weeks searching the island's woods and marshes for mosquitoes to study, though all he really had to do was step outside of any building on the island at any time. The Moss-Skweetos closely observed Mills during his studies and saw that he was a robust, educated man. They agreed that he could be a possible candidate, or vessel, for their mind control virus. Some bugs believed that he might not become feverish and appear crazy, like Elijah James, and they considered that he had all the right qualities that could finally make the virus work.

One day, as Dr. Mills roamed across Assateague, he stood in a knee deep pool of murky standing marsh water. The bugs bedeviled him, trying to infect him with a message of first contact. He swatted at them, but they dodged and came at him again and again, from all directions. He killed a dozen on his arm, but three dozen took their place. He ran away from the cloud, but the bugs followed him, or he simply ran into another cloud of bugs. He soon found that he had no recourse against them.

"How do people live like this?" He asked, his arms flailing uncontrollably. But then, Elijah James came to mind. Dr. Mills squatted in the swampy pool. He reached down, shoveled up two handfuls of mud, and slathered it over every inch of his exposed skin. He created a barrier that the bugs, try as they might, found impenetrable. Dr. Mills felt immediate relief: the bugs couldn't bite him any more, plus the mud felt cool and supple. He found that looking like a mud caked mad-man allowed him to go back to his studies mostly undisturbed. He understood how to cope a little better with the bugs, and he also understood Elijah James a little better. From then on, whenever he stepped outside to roam around Chincoteauge, or Assateague, he smeared on the mud. The townsfolk sighed and shook their heads, believing they now had a second town lunatic.

    Tuesdays were always slow at Don's Seafood Restaurant, and that's why they established their Two for Tuesday lunch special: two sides with a sandwich instead of one. Customers liked this deal, and in turn, they returned for lunch on any given Tuesday; for french fries and hush puppies, or cole slaw and hush puppies, or homemade potato chips and hush puppies. Apparently, people liked hush puppies. What customers never realized was that they were getting half portions of each side dish, equaling exactly the same amount of food they would have received had they ordered just one side dish. Nevertheless this approach worked, and it worked on Darryl Baker too. He would drive across the causeway every Tuesday at 11:45a.m. for hush puppies, and also to unwittingly make puppy dog eyes at Molly.

    Sometimes as Darryl drove down the causeway, his mind wandered from thoughts of Molly toward the engineering accomplishment of lining the causeway with a string of billboards anchored into soft alluvial mud. The billboards were worn and tattered and the woodwork had been bleached gray by the sun. They had evidently been there for decades, so Darryl surmised that they must have been constructed at a time when humans had only more pedestrian technologies. Darryl's mind went to work; "A: Someone floated a shallow draft barge full of telephone pole sized posts to the location where they wanted to build a sign. B: Workers used a simple barge mounted crane to hoist the poles vertically in place. C: Men pile-drove the poles into the mud by hand. D: Once all of the poles were in place, the workers built a frame and then a flat surface. E: The entire frame helped stabilize the poles in the highly unstable mud. F: A billboard man was then free to paste advertisements onto the assembly." This process made logical sense to Darryl.

Occasionally Darryl would see a man actually gluing a new advertisement to a billboard. This set Darryl's engineering mind to work figuring out the necessary steps; "A: Load a Jon-boat with all necessary tools, environmentally safe glues, and swaths of a printed paper advertisement. B: Float a Jon-boat to the predetermined billboard. C: anchor the boat on three axis, so the boat won't float away, and so it will be a stable base of operations. D: Ready all necessary tools, environmentally safe glues and printed advertisement. E: Smear environmentally safe glue over old advertisement and unfurl new paper advertisement across flat surface. F: Squeegee out all trapped air bubbles from beneath paper surface."

Darryl loved imagining process, because that's the way his mind was wired; B followed A, C followed B, D followed C. A must be complete before moving on to B, and there was no way to proceed to C if B had not been implemented, and so on, all the way to Z. This was Darryl's thought process every time he saw the billboard man carrying out his business, and this was his thought process regarding just about everything he encountered in life. And this is why Darryl, who could accurately define the probable distribution of a quantum state experiment, was incapable of registering anything that life produced that wasn't logically sequential, which was pretty much everything that life produced: including aliens.

Though Two for Tuesdays became one of the busiest days at Don's Seafood Restaurant, Mondays were still Mondays. It was the slowest day of the week for Don's, just as it is the slowest day of the week for most restaurants. It was so slow that Don's didn't even try to create a day of the week deal, like Two for Tuesdays. Plus, no one could come up with a catchy slogan for Monday. So, Monday just stayed Monday.

Molly rang an order of fish and chips, plus a soda, into the computer. "Cover me luv," she said to the only other waitress working on a God-forsaken Monday. "I'm taking lunch," she added. Molly poured herself a soda and went downstairs to hang around the kitchen until her fish and chips were ready. She leaned back on the brushed metal food service counter, arms crossed, bored, taking a dim view of the mostly empty dining room, and of her mostly empty life. A fry cook set a grease soaked white paper bag on the counter.

"Fish and Chips," he called out.

Molly replied, "Thanks luv," grabbed her lunch and scooted out the back door. The moment she stepped outside, bugs immediately attacked the spider web tattoo on her neck. She dashed across the parking lot swatting the bugs over and over, but they kept attacking the tattoo. She trotted into Waterfront Park, just catty-corner behind Don's Seafood Restaurant, where Molly headed for the only covered pavilion in the area. An ever present breeze coming off the water by the pavilion was often sufficient to whisk away attacking bugs from Molly and her spider web tattoo. She set the bag on a picnic table, plopped down on the bench seat, pulled her fish and chips from the bag and started eating. She liked to have lunch under the pavilion. She could be alone. She gazed out over the water, and, mesmerized by the sounds of small waves sloshing against the dock and the boats, she forgot about work and the stupid things that provincial life threw at her each day. Molly slipped into a daydream.

    Immense strangler tree roots cascade over the cornices of an ancient stone temple, like an octopus jealously gripping its prey. Moss cloaked walls, turn drab, time-stained granite to into lush jungle verdigris. Molly high-steps over a threshold into the building. Macaques chirp, echoing through the halls. Molly has been told to avoid the aggressive little monkeys, but she's crossed the world to explore Angkor Wat, so she presses on. Descending through a corridor, she caresses abrasive stone reliefs of Hindu deities. Water drops from the ceiling and plunks into puddles around her feet. Molly turns a corner and crepuscular rays stream through holes in the collapsed ceiling, spotlighting a stone likeness of Vishnu, who is draped in saffron robes and shielded from the elements by a glowing tangerine umbrella. Molly is nearly moved to tears by its beauty. She hears the Macaques coming closer, like they know where she is. Monkey chirps bounce off the walls from all directions. They are closing in. Chirps become chatter. Chatter become shrieks, and shrieks become a cacophony of quacks. Quacks?

    Molly reemerged into reality, and regrettably found herself once again under the pavilion. Across the park an old woman sat on a bench under a trellis.

Needy ducks mobbed her, begging for a handout. The old woman happily obliged. That's why she was there: to feed the ducks. Just beyond the old woman, Molly spotted an older couple, husband and wife, who were obviously tourists. She had waited on them the prior Saturday at Don's because they sat at Darryl's table by the window. The wife had oysters, the husband had the crab imperial. The old couple climbed around on a set of four patently oversized Adirondack chairs. They were built and placed there by the Department of Tourism, so tourists would sit on the chairs, take pictures of themselves and then show the pictures to all of their friends. It was a clever and cheap way to advertise Chincoteague: by making the target of the ads, responsible for the creation and distribution of the ads. On the backrests of each chair was a letter; L,O,V, and E. The husband sat on the E chair, and though he was six feet tall, his feet dangled in the air like a toddler. The wife jumped down, focused her camera on the man and goaded him to smile. Instead, he made a pouty face, like a petulant child. The wife laughed and took the picture anyway. The department of tourism conspiracy was working.

"Oh, God!" Molly muttered, glaring at the old couple playing cutesy. She couldn't imagine doing this with Lucas. She gobbled up lunch, inadvertently giving herself break-time to spare, so she just sat at the table, avoided work, and dwelled on her boring life. Molly set an elbow on the table, rested her chin into the palm of her hand and sighed. She turned toward the Main Street entrance to the park where the town had long ago erected a statue of the wild pony, Misty of Chincoteauge, the island's most famous resident. The statue idealized a frolicking mare; flaring her nostrils, her mane flying in the breeze and her tail whipping side to side. A high spirited pony, for sure, frozen in perpetual motion. But this statue is a lie. It's the way everyone wants to remember Misty, even though she spent most of her life idly standing around, nose to the ground, munching grass.

Molly complained, "Someone should write a story about me. Then they could put my statue in the park." Her chin slumped further into her palm, "Waitress extraordinaire," she groaned. "This place is boring! Why am I here when there are so many exotic places on the planet!"

At that very moment, confectionary scientist Mahesh Venkatachalam and his family crossed the arched bridge at the end of the causeway onto Chincoteague Island. Mahesh had spent a lifetime scrimping and saving his money so that one day he could leave his boring little village in Darjeeling, India in order to see first hand, the storied Chincoteague Island, the far-flung home of the wild pony Misty, whom he had read and dreamt about as a child. Mahesh and his family pressed their noses against the car windows, taking it all in. Each of them eager and smiling that they had arrived at this alien destination. Mahesh couldn't believe his luck, that he was finally here. He would not be disappointed, though he didn't understand what most of us don't understand, and what Molly definitely didn't understand: everywhere is exotic, when you're not from there.

A few blocks away, back at Waterfront Park, one very strong bug successfully fought the wind and landed right on Molly's spider web tattoo. It then bit her hard. "Bastard!," she yelped. If Molly had paid attention, she would have noticed that the bugs rarely bit her anywhere else on her body. They always zeroed in on the spider web tattoo on the side of her neck. Little did Molly know, even though she always focused a world away, that the Moss-Skweetos' sworn enemy on their home world is a race of venomous, eight-legged, multi-eyed, web spinning beasts, best described to you and me, as spiders. The Moss-Skweetos have been in perpetual war with the spiders since time began. Spiders catching and killing bugs, and bugs killing spiders. Imagine the Moss-Skweetos disappointment as they crash landed on Earth, only to discover that spiders were already there. Through the ages, the war continued on Earth, and naturally, whenever the bugs saw Molly's tattoo, they attacked it.

    The breeze off of the water died down, giving more bugs the chance to wage war on Molly, the older couple, and the duck lady, who all began fighting off the Moss-Skweetos. "Stupid bugs!" Molly swatted and swatted, but eventually gave up. She snatched up her trash and dashed across the park toward the indoor safety of Don's, which was the last place she wanted to be. "Get me outta here!" She snapped. "Somewhere without friggin' bugs! Anywhere!" Molly swatted and swatted, killing bug after bug, not knowing that she was murdering the only life forms on the planet that were potentially capable of taking her anywhere she wanted to go throughout the universe.

The next day, it was Two for Tuesdays again at Don's Seafood Restaurant. The hostess sat Darryl at his favorite table by the window, overlooking Queen Sound Channel. Molly was lost in a picture of Angkor Wat again when the hostess breezed by the waitress station. "Your boyfriend is here," she said. Molly snapped out of her daydream, poured a glass of half/half iced tea, put on the best smile she could manage and glided to Darryl's table.

"Mornin' luv," she said placing the glass and a straw on the table in front of Darryl.

"Hey." He said. "Thanks."

"Half/half right?," Molly asked.

"Yeah. Sure."

"How's stuff going today?"

"Oh, you know," Darryl searched for a witty answer, "it's stuff." He said. "Stuff is stuff."

"It is. Isn't it?" Molly agreed, and seeing that the small talk was going nowhere, she got back to business. "The usual?," she asked.

Darryl nodded. "Sounds great."

"Alright luv," she said, "I'll be right back with your order."

He watched Molly glide away, though as usual, he pretended not to.

Darryl tapped the end of his straw on the table and pulled it out of its paper wrapper. He slid the straw into his drink and then nervously killed time by twisting the wrapper until it was a tightly wound string. Molly returned with a heaping plate of crab imperial, fries, and a bottle of ketchup. She set it in front of Darryl.

"Here you go luv."

"Thanks," he said.

"Everything look good?"

"Great," he replied.

"Great." Molly said. She almost pivoted to return to the waitress station and the picture of Angkor Wat that she cut out of a stolen magazine, but this time something kept her at the table.

"You like the crab imperial, don't you?"

"Yeah," Darryl replied, unfolding a napkin onto his lap.

"You know, you've been here every Tuesday for a while now, and you know, I still don't know your name."

Darryl was back on his heels: she was asking him for his name. "Oh," he said, "Darryl" and he extended a hand to shake.

Molly grasped his hand and shook it, "Molly." she said.

"Yeah I know," Darryl replied, but immediately regretted it.

"Yeah?" Molly asked.

Darryl pointed, "your name tag."

Molly chuckled, a little relieved and a little embarrassed. "Yeah," she caressed the tag below her collarbone. And then she asked, "You live on the island?"

"On the Delmarva," he replied

Molly briefly thought to mention that she too lived on the Delmarva, but thought better to divulge this to a semi-strange man with puppy dog eyes. Molly might have to also then admit that she lives in a crappy rented trailer on a swampy little lot, which she was simply too embarrassed to talk about.

She pivoted, "What do you do?"

"What?" He asked.

"You know, for a living."

"Oh." Darryl said, and then pointed out the window, "I work over there."

"At Wallops?" Molly was surprised to find herself genuinely impressed, and interested. Nothing on the Delmarva nor the island impressed or interested her.

"Yeah." Darryl nodded.

"Doing what?"

"Well," Darryl reflected for a moment. "Do you see the biggest satellite dish over there?"

"Yeah."

"That's what I do. I'm in charge of it."

"What does it do?" Molly asked.

"It looks into space," he said. "It looks for alien life."

"Wow!" Molly exclaimed. "Like a telescope?"

"Yeah," Darryl answered, "kinda. Pretty much."

"Found any aliens?" Molly teased Darryl.

"Oh," he nodded, "no."

Molly prodded him further, "Is this super secret info you can't tell me, or are you just not lookin' in the right place, luv?"

"Nooo," he assured her, "no secret. No, I guess you're right, we just haven't looked in the right place." He then hesitated, "I mean, the universe is a big place. We look pretty far into space—billions of light years away."

"Why so far?" she asked. "Why not look closer?"

"Um, you know, close is relative in space. I look close too. You know, I'm looking all over. I do want to find alien life. My paycheck kinda depends on it."

"Yeah, well," she said, "How likely is that? I mean, I want to travel around the world, but I don't expect it will happen."

"Mmmm, right," Darryl became a little defensive, "you know, I wrote my dissertation on this very question. At this point we don't expect to discover aliens. Nothing's imminent, because we haven't found any proof that they exist."

"Hmm," she nodded, and then she asked, "Well, how would you know if you are lookin' at 'em?"

Darryl assured her, "Oh, we'd know."

"Like how?"

"Uhhhh, you know, finding evidence that they'd used some sort of technology, sound, visible light, infrared, ultraviolet, xray, gamma radiation, stuff like that."

Molly seemed dissatisfied with his answer. Maybe she just didn't understand it, or maybe she did.

"What if the aliens don't use any of that stuff?" She asked.

"Well the probability is that any intelligent life would use something like…"

Molly interrupted, "Yeah, but," she said, "what if they don't?"

"Um…"

Molly continued, "I mean, xrays and stuff. That's stuff we use, right? What if they use other stuff: stuff that we haven't even thought of yet? Stuff we don't even have a name for. And if you don't know it exists, how would you even think to look for it?" In Molly's ignorance, she managed to ask all the relevant scientific questions that Darryl never thought to ask, due to his own well educated ignorance. In Darryl's process driven mind, B follows A, and C follows B and so on, so since he was basically only at E follows D in the alien finding process, why ask questions about X, Y and Z? How could those questions even be conceivable without the answers to U, V, and W? And here was Molly, unencumbered by a PhD, asking those very questions.

Molly paused, cocked her head, raised an eyebrow, scrunched her lips, and then asked the one question so out of logical order that Darryl was utterly incapable of even registering it in his wildest dreams.

"And then," she said, "what happens once you find 'em?"

Tourists, by nature, don't stay in one place very long. The older couple at Waterfront Park, those two whose cutesiness turned Molly's stomach, the older couple who Molly served crab imperial and oysters at Don's Seafood Restaurant, were typical tourists. So, they often moved around the island to see stuff.

By Wednesday, Molly drove through town to work. She was so mired in her own misery that she never noticed the old couple milling about in the parking lot of the bike rental shop. The old man helped his wife spray an over-abundance of bug spray on her arms and legs, as well as a fine mist overhead. She did the same for him. They knew full well that they were engulfing each other with poison, though that didn't matter if it killed bugs or just kept them away.

They launched their rented bikes onto the road and headed for the beach. The old couple casually pedaled their cruisers across a bridge into Assateague Island National Wildlife Refuge. Almost immediately they began to notice bugs landing on their arms and faces and any other place skin was exposed. They discovered that when they pedaled harder, and went faster, the bugs were less likely to latch on: kind of a reverse venturi, if such a thing exists. They stopped a few places along the way, like the visitor center, where inside, they enjoyed the air conditioning, and the exhibits, but mostly the air conditioning, and the absence fo bugs. They walked around feigning interest in the stuffed animals and the dioramas, and even read a few signs about life within the refuge. But they ignored a very large kiosk sporting a modernist profile of a bug. They passed the kiosk, indifferent, since they really didn't care to read or learn about bugs, because what good were bugs, except for killing?

They left the building and its air conditioning, and were immediately attacked by throngs of the little devils. The old couple showered each other with another round of bug spray, got on their bikes, and pedaled hard and fast to avoid the bugs. Closer to the beach, they came across a quaint old lighthouse and the keeper's residence. The wife wanted to stop and see it. They parked their bikes on a rack near a federally funded and constructed pit toilet, doused themselves with more bug spray and hiked through a low lying pine forest toward the lighthouse. Pine scent permeated everything, even pleasantly overcoming the chemical funk of bug spray mixed with sweat. But no matter how much poison they sprayed on themselves, the bugs attacked. Down the length of the entire trail they faced a Moss-Skweeto onslaught, horde after horde, all seemingly resistant, if not wholly immune to the bug spray. The old man and his wife gave up, sprinted back to their bikes, frantically added more useless bug spray and escaped as quickly as they could. But the bugs that attacked the old couple weren't immune to the spray. Not at all. They landed on the old couple, they were poisoned, they died, and when they fell more came to take their place because it was their duty to carry out attacks and even suicide missions for the greater good: to protect a vital, imminent Moss-Skweeto mission.

Behind the pit toilet, the low lying pine forest remained flooded with murky, green, stagnant water, throughout the year, even in dry times. It was especially suited for Moss-Skweetos to live, breed, eat, and work. It was a perfect stronghold, and it became their most important base of operations. For generations, the best and brightest bugs assembled in the flooded pine forest to develop a strategy to leave Earth. After years of preparation, today was the day for action.

 The bugs assembled a commando swarm and set off among the cover of woods, streaming through the trees like rivers flow between rocks. They crossed the bridge over into Chincoteague, flying low, strafing houses and downtown businesses, losing some operatives to the occasional swat, bug spray, or windshield. The swarm successfully advanced to Waterfront Park, and to the docks, where they faced their biggest challenge: crossing Queen Sound Channel. The bugs surged up the causeway, fighting an unexpectedly strong headwind, exhausting many, and further reducing their ranks. The lead bugs pressed the others to continue for the greater good. If they could make it to the Delmarva, they could make it to the other side of the universe. But by this point the swarm had thinned so much that many considered retreating back to base. They argued that at this rate of attrition, they wouldn't have enough left to carry out their mission, and they would have to start all over again. But they bravely pressed on.

Something was wrong. Darryl leaned toward his computer monitor as if doing so would help him better understand what was happening. He squinted at a series of squiggly lines drawn across the screen by a computer program that he himself devised, and then created. The lines were designed to represent broadcast radiation that traveled across the expanse of space and intersected the Earth, where they were picked up and extracted from the air by Darryl's large parabolic antenna at Wallops. They were then interpreted by his computer program and displayed on the screen as incoming sound. Only now, as Darryl leaned in toward his computer screen, he could see that they clearly didn't look like incoming sound. They looked more like the beginnings of outgoing sound, like a transmitter signal. But this wasn't possible.

"Huh," Darryl grunted.

He stepped away from his desk and stood in the doorway of his office. He looked one way down the hall, and then looked the other way. He then blankly stared across the hall at what he now knew was Dave's office. He could hear the faint repeated clicking of a computer mouse. Darryl marched across the hall and poked his head in the doorway.

"Hey," he hesitated, "Dave?"

"Yes?" Dave cocked his head back to peer down his nose through half moon reading glasses. He didn't bother to look at Darryl, but instead remained focused on his computer screen. He was the very model of a busy NASA scientist doing important NASA stuff on his computer: except that he wasn't. He had heard Darryl approaching his office and quickly hid his game of solitaire, which he played all day every day, unless someone approached his office. So now, Dave appeared busy, as Darryl entered the room to hover by his desk.

"Hey, um, are you running anything on the Extra Terrestrial Telescope?"

"Running anything?"

"Yeah, you know, like trying to broadcast something through it?"

"I don't think so," Dave replied sarcastically.

"Can you check?"

"It's not something I would do." Dave wasn't lying, because solitaire was the only thing he did at work.

You see, Dave used to be a talented scientist. He specialized in engineering processes, you know, D follows C, which follows B, which follows A. He was especially good at this, much more so than Darryl and many other engineers. This is because Dave has a remarkably tight sphincter, much more so than Darryl, and many other engineers. As a result, Dave's work, the process of doing anything or making anything, was ruled by his sphincter. Even Dave's personal life was ruled by his remarkably tight sphincter. He was always on a schedule: awake at 5:30, out of bed at 5:31, going to the bathroom at 5:32, oatmeal and orange juice at 5:35, and, well, you get the picture. His sphincter ruled him throughout the day, relaxing only at 3pm, on the nose, in order to let go of yesterday's oatmeal and other contents.

But, Dave's sphincter was also his ruin at NASA. He was so inflexible about processes, that over the years, his NASA cohorts became frustrated with him, and no longer wanted to work with him, so nobody did, and he became a desk jockey. The problem was, everyone felt kind of sorry for pushing Dave aside, and no one readily admitted to the administration that they were no longer using him for their own projects. So, every day, for years, Dave unlocked the door of his office at 8:30 sharp, launched his solitaire program at 8:32 and spent most of his day sorting digital playing cards on his computer until 10a.m. when he stretched his legs by taking a lap around the outside of the building, and then at 3pm, when his sphincter relaxed. None of the brilliant scientists and engineers at NASA were smart enough to comprehend how Dave spent his day, or how useless he had become. Maybe they just preferred to ignore this fact, by ignoring him. The only real interaction anyone had with Dave was when they left their desk to ask Dave a question, just as Darryl did.

"Well, can you still check?"

Dave continued to click and type away at his computer just as he was doing when Darryl walked in. "Nope. Not doing anything with the E.T. Telescope."

"Did you actually ch.."

"Just did."

Unconvinced, Darryl prodded him further, "so you didn't put an amplifier on the antenna to transmit something?"

Dave finally stopped typing and looked at Darryl over his half moon glasses. "Nope," he said, knowing full well that he hadn't done anything of use at Wallops in at least a decade.

"Okay, thanks," Darryl conceded and then shambled down the hallway carefully ruminating about the problem with his telescope. He was doing exactly, it seems, what engineers and scientists tend to do when faced with a conundrum: they pace. Darryl wandered, theorizing this and rationalizing that, so lost in thought that he wandered outside the building without even realizing it.

"What could cause a receiver to suddenly become a transmitter?" he wondered. This made no sense. This wasn't possible in Darryl's A-B-C concept of the world.

His ears began to ring. No, it was more like a high pitched whine, and it grew louder and louder. He jostled his head to shake off the noise, but instead, the whine was in full force now. Darryl suddenly found himself face to face with a million or more bugs coating his Extra Terrestrial Telescope.

"Whoaa!" Darryl groaned. He tried to wipe some bugs off with his hands, but he was quickly overwhelmed by attacking Moss-Skweetos who bit and bit and bit him. He frantically brushed them off his arm, smearing blood and guts down his forearm, but they just kept coming after him. He ran inside, and barreled down the halls until he found a janitor's closet. He rummaged through the contents looking for a can of bug spray, but settled instead on a push broom. Back outside, he scrubbed the bugs off his precious telescope, which provoked them to swarm Darryl with an even greater ferocity. He flailed his arms and swatted the air, smacking the bugs who landed on his cheeks and forehead and any exposed skin, but this too, proved futile, and again, he retreated inside.

Darryl scurried through the building to track down Henry, the facilities manager. Soon, both Darryl and Henry were standing at the base of the telescope, Henry holding a one gallon pump sprayer filled with insecticide. Henry pressurized the tank by pumping the pump, pointed the wand and pulled the trigger, waving it from side to side across the body of the telescope. Some bugs fell dead to the ground, but many more counter-attacked, driving Henry and Darryl back inside again. A small squadron of bugs pursued Darryl and Henry, infiltrating the building. Some attacked, but many peppered themselves on the walls, preparing to pounce. Darryl paced, fuming and hysterical, and pointed at the bugs, "Get them off my telescope," he shouted at Henry, "Kill them all."

Here's where I remind you yet again that words mean stuff. And though words mean certain stuff to one person, they might mean something else to another person. It is the difference between imply and infer, which are often confused by people who think these two words actually mean the same thing. They don't.

When Darryl said, "kill them all," his meaning was actually somewhat vague. He meant that he wanted Henry to kill all of the Moss-Skweetos on the telescope, but since he didn't specifically state his intentions, he was therefore implying these intentions. When Henry heard Darryl say, "kill them all," he reasoned that Darryl meant exactly what he said, that he was being specific, specifically, that he wanted to kill all the Moss-Skweetos everywhere. Henry inferred that Darryl's intentions were much broader in scope than even Darryl imagined. It was from this simple misunderstanding that Henry also inferred he was now empowered to do what he did next.

Henry resurrected two old tank trucks on the back lot at Wallops. They had once been used to carry 100 low lead fuel across the aviation ramp to all of the old piston powered NASA aircraft. But as NASA began to use more and more jets, the trucks became irrelevant. Since people don't like to throw away perfectly good irrelevant things, the trucks were parked on the back lot to slowly rust away and become even more irrelevant. But, Henry saw them and knew how he could use them.

As the head groundsman, Henry lorded over a substantial amount of money to do things that he often wanted to do. It helped that he was surrounded by a bunch of tight-sphinctered engineers whose job it was to think up unimaginably crazy ideas and turn them into unimaginably expensive projects that might, or might not, accomplish something. Henry's idea was to convert the old tanker trucks into pest control spray trucks. It was yet another idea that might, or might not accomplish something, but relatively speaking, not unimaginably crazy, nor unimaginably expensive. So as Henry converted the old fuel trucks into pest control spray trucks, no one at Wallops paid very much attention.

As the trucks were restored and outfitted with hoses and misting nozzles, Darryl researched insecticides, and developed his very own formula for bug-poison. Though not technically a chemist, he made a particularly deadly concoction. From then on, when the bugs infested Darryl's telescope, and they infested it many times, Henry started up the spray truck and spread toxic fog around the telescope and across the entire grounds at Wallops. No one minded, except the bugs, who were killed in droves, instantly poisoned as they flew, dead before they hit the ground. The bugs hated Henry, but they despised Darryl.

When Darryl shouted, "kill them all," in the hallway, he was overheard by the bugs who chased him into the building. And like Henry, the Moss-Skweetos also inferred that, "kill them all," meant exactly what Darryl said, rather than what he implied. This interpretation spread throughout the Moss-Skweeto population, and Darryl became public enemy number one: a genocidal maniac, a Hitler, a Mengele, a Stalin, a Pol Pot.

Henry whose sphincter was much more relaxed than any of his NASA engineer cohorts, was just as motivated to tinker and to build and to create, just for the sake of doing so, and to see if something could be made to happen. After repeatedly wiping out clouds of bugs at Wallops, Henry felt satisfied that his spray trucks were a success. But Henry's motivated sphincter was, at the same time, dissatisfied that his success was confined to only a few hundred acres. Moreover, Darryl had asked Henry to, "kill them all," at least that's what he inferred.

Before too long, Henry carted a drum of bug spray through the old airplane hangar at Wallops. There he spotted the Beech 18. It was an old twin engine taildragger that had become irrelevant in the jet age, but not irrelevant enough to discard. Henry had a crazy idea, but knew there wasn't enough money in his own buildings and grounds budget to realize a crazy idea that might or might not accomplish something.

So, at the next town council meeting, Henry proposed a new tax to pay for the restoration of the old airplane and its conversion to a spray plane; a crop duster essentially, but one that sprayed its poison in a fine mist over the town, instead of over a cornfield. He reasoned to the council, that especially in the summertime, bugs continuously clouded the air, and constantly tormented people on Chincoteague and Assateague. And then he reasoned that in the summer, most of those tormented people were tourists who didn't go on vacation to be eaten alive by bugs. If the bugs were gone, he suggested, then more tourists would come. And more tourists bring more money, and more money means more tax dollars, some of which could be used to spray a poison mist over both islands to, "kill them all."

The city council nodded their collective heads, and before too long the Beech 18 was shined up, and the words, "Pest Control" were painted on its fuselage. Every morning, just as people were sipping their coffee, the plane strafed the treetops in carefully coordinated swaths, releasing its toxin, killing millions of bugs, and infinitesimally poisoning the rest of the island's inhabitants. What the plane didn't kill with poison, it murdered as it flew through swarms, their lives inescapably sacrificed on the blunt nose of the fuselage, the wing leading edge, or the meat grinding propeller.

Chincoteauge Bugs

Chincoteague Bugs

splatten' on the windshield, streakin' with guts

get 'em on your wings

get 'em on your prop

coated too thick and your plane is gonna drop

They are former little Chincoteague bugs

    But it soon became apparent that of the two islands, there was only enough money to spray Chincoteague, because of the two islands, that's where all of the taxpayers lived and vacationed. No one on Chincoteague could figure out how to tax the wild animals on Assateague, so they could pay for their share of the pest control program. Moreover, none of those taxpaying residents of Chincoteague wanted their money to fund the bug free comfort of a bunch of tax evading, wild animals over on Assateague. The money, therefore, didn't leave the shores of Chincoteague, and neither did the insecticide.

    Henry failed to, "kill them all," but that didn't stop Henry's bug control program. Like most people, Henry shrugged and conveniently forgot his initial goal when he realized his failure was fully funded "as is." The taxpayers on Chincoteague were happy to dole out the dollars to keep the scourge of bugs away from the residents and the tourists, and as long as the tourism dollars kept coming, Henry was perfectly happy to forget the phrase, "kill them all." The bugs were, therefore, safe from Henry's motivated sphincter, at least those who kept to Assateague, which were most of them. Henry had unwittingly created a de facto sanctuary there for the Moss-Skweetos. This haven gave the bugs the time and the opportunity to breed and grow their numbers in the swamps, to devise an escape from the Earth, and to plot their revenge against the dreaded Darryl.

    The bugs meticulously surveilled Darryl Baker to better understand his habits. They contemplated several ways to communicate with him, much like enemy states opening back channels to keep from annihilating each other with world-obliterating missiles. The bugs soon became aware that Darryl spent a great deal of his time at his desk analyzing information sent to his computer screen from his Extra Terrestrial Telescope. So at first, a small group of bugs swarmed the telescope and took control of it to try to parley with him. And, Darryl actually did receive the message: a squiggly line that popped up on his computer screen. But the bugs' message didn't match Darryl's narrow concept of what a message from aliens would look like. So, it didn't just go unnoticed, he chose to ignore it by shutting down his computer and going to lunch.

    When a the bugs tried to bypass Darryl, taking control of his telescope to call home, they had crossed an imaginary dotted line into Darryl's perceived territory, resulting in his edict to, "kill them all." So they couldn't attempt to commandeer his telescope any longer without great danger to their operatives and possibly their entire species. They were then forced to find other ways to contact to him. The bugs spied on him for several months and a pattern soon emerged: every Tuesday Darryl drove across the causeway to Chincoteague for lunch. This gave the bugs another idea.

A squadron of Moss-Skweetos were sent to the workshop of John James, who Darryl knew only as the billboard man. John's family had resided on Chincoteague for generations. As a matter of fact, John still lived on the original family land grant secured back in the late 18th century by his great-great-great grandfather, Elijah James. A group of commando bugs infiltrated John's workshop where they found him leaning over a large drafting table creating billboard ads. They attacked him, bit hard and locked on. Before he was able to swat and kill them, a few managed to infect him with their mind control virus. John James appeared to be a suitable candidate. The bugs designed this particular virus to travel to John's brain with a message which he would then relay to Darryl. They would have infected Darryl directly with a message, but they didn't believe his A-B-C structured engineer's mind was suitable for the virus. The bugs just didn't have faith Darryl would infer the correct message implied by a virus: sometimes a virus could just be too subtle. They would need to speak to him simply, in his own language, and in logical order.

Complicating matters more, the bugs didn't know that Elijah James' very peculiar DNA, which was resistant to the mind control virus, and produced odd results, had been passed down through generations of James' descendants, all the way to John James. The virus worked its way through John's body up to his brain, while the James DNA fought and corrupted the message every bit along the way. John grew feverish, and a little delirious, but diligently still came to work. At his shop, he then imbedded the bugs' message into the next batch of advertisements, which he then plastered on the causeway billboards.

The next Two for Tuesdays, Darryl drove down the causeway and noticed a freshly papered sign, "Please drive safely: do not pass on the causeway!" And then he saw three more new installations in a row, "For the best soft serve, stop at Mr. Wippy!" followed by, "Killing time? Rent a moped today at Fun on Wheels," and lastly, "Chincoteague honors our local U.S. Veterans."

The bugs message to Darryl, now in big bold letters on big bold sequentially placed signs, was simply written and plain to see, for him and for everyone else driving down the causeway. But, the James' family resistance to the virus ensured that it was obscured to anyone with common sense. John was unable to articulate the message on only one sign. Instead, he fragmented the words randomly across the four new billboards. And, because Darryl's mind was uncompromisingly wired only for A-B-C order, and was therefore, unable to detect randomness or nonconformity, he was unable to recognize that the signs were a direct plea for him to, "Please stop killing us."

If you're old enough, and I'm not saying I am, but I'm old enough to remember the famous children's book Misty of Chincoteague. Misty was a light brown painted pony that lived quietly and happily on Assateague Island. One day, Misty heard a rustling in the brush. The next thing she knew, men on horses were chasing her through the swamp. They chased her through the woods, all the way to the island's edge. There, she was forced to swim across a channel of water, trotted through town and abruptly penned up at the fairgrounds to be auctioned off to the highest bidder. The person that offered the most money for Misty turned out to be author Marguerite Henry. She named the pony Misty, who by the way, had previously called herself, Hell Bitch.

Now that's not exactly how it all happened, but it's good enough for fiction, which is what Marguerite then did: she wrote a book about Misty of Chincoteague. The book was an instant hit. It sold enough copies that influential people in Hollywood decided that Misty was not just a pony, but a cash cow, and therefore, worthy of her own movie. Her story might make millions, and they wouldn't have to pay a penny of royalties to Misty. So, Hollywood made Misty a star. Her movie premiered world-wide at the Island Roxie on Chincoteague. A barrage of paparazzi showed up: flash bulbs ignited as promoters cast Misty's hoof prints in wet concrete near the box office. Misty made the island famous, just as the bugs did again during the great swarm of 2016, though no one wrote a book about them, or made a movie about them, or cast their feet in wet concrete.

Building on the success of Hell Bitch's capture and conversion to Misty the movie star, Chincoteague residents have, every year, rounded up some of the wild ponies on Assateague, and auctioned them off: something they still do. Tourists love the ponies. Us townsfolk just think they're ill tempered unwashed beasts. Coincidentally, so do the Moss-Skweetos, who by and large, leave the ponies alone, that is, unless they get really hungry.

Assateague bugs

Assateague bugs

Belly full of nothin' cause there's nothin' to grub

landin' on the ponies

to suckle and feed

gotta be starvin' cause they're stinky and mean

They are, hungry little Assateague bugs

Anyways, Misty still lives on the Island, though her current condition can accurately be described as "stuffed and on display."

But how did the wild ponies get on the island in the first place?

In 1962, a particularly violent nor-easter hit the islands. The storm flooded everything, and destroyed much of the town. It reminded everyone how vulnerable and prone the islands were to such storms. But, the townsfolk didn't need much reminding.

Romanticized stories tell us that about three hundred years before the '62 nor-easter, a similarly violent nor-easter hit Assateague. Off the coast, a Spanish galleon loaded with conquistadors and their ponies, suffered through solid sheets of rain and raging winds as their small wooden ship bobbed helplessly among the crests and troughs of an angry ocean. Officers sequestered themselves within their quarters, while sailors were forced to ride out the storm on the top deck, lashing themselves to masts, or anything solid enough to keep them from being washed overboard by storm surge. The ponies, agitated and terrified in the cargo hold, neighed and whinnied and kicked and screamed out of fear of this unknown force that literally upended their world. Romanticized stories tell us that the winds and waves of the brutal storm thrust the galleon onto a sandbar, shipwrecking it there. The ponies, desperate to live, narrowly escaped their bondage from the ship's hold, and through sheer will to survive, they braved the fury of the sea and swam ashore. The herd dragged themselves onto the beach, rose to their feet, and pummeled by whipping winds, they stumbled inland among the dunes of Assateague Island. The lead pony, tired and weatherbeaten, found a place protected from the wind, where he lied down. The other ponies followed, and they all sheltered together for the night. This was the foundation for a centuries old colony of Spanish ponies. It's a splendid lie.

Critics point out that it would be nearly impossible for a herd of ponies to achieve such a self rescue, since during such a violent storm, someone onboard a ship usually gives a command to "batten down the hatches," thus securing, or locking everything in the cargo hold, which in this case, would have included many doomed ponies.

The romantics countered this skepticism saying that when the ship hit the sandbar it cracked open like an egg. The ponies spilled out like the white and the yolk, and were therefore, able to swim to their freedom.

The critics then pointed out that ships tend to crack open like an egg on rocks, not sandbars, and there are no rocks in this part of the ocean, and that sand isn't nearly as jagged and sharp as a rock. And, to make the point even finer, they asked why did the ponies survive, but the people didn't? Surely, they would have, and if they did, for three hundred years, people on Chincoteague would have spoken Spanish instead of English. It's nearly impossible, they say, that the ponies could have arrived on the island this way.

But, then the romantics smugly pointed out that "words mean stuff." They argued that the words "nearly impossible," don't mean the same thing as, "impossible."

The controversy over the ponies origin raged for more than a century. But, eventually a third party joined the debate: retired people. Bored, with too much time on their hands, certain old people spent many tedious, lonely hours pouring over land deeds, and bills of sale, and trusts, and what not in the local county courthouses. They did all this, because often near the end of a person's life, they strangely become interested in what led to their own beginning. So, they go to the courthouse to engage in genealogy: life's last hobby. When the amateur genealogists on Chincoteague and the Delmarva tried to piece together their own existence, they stumbled across the most probable and logical reason for the ponies existence on Assateague: tax evasion.

    Early laws of the Delmarva empowered the government to tax personal property that was part of the peninsula, or that was on the peninsula. This included ponies. The white, wealthy, land-owning, tax-adverse farmers and businessmen on the peninsula, people we now call Republicans, were loathe to pay taxes on their own riches, believing that taxes should be paid only by those stupid enough to be honest. The Republicans on the peninsula read the law carefully, and read it over and over again until they understood that the words, "taxed on the peninsula," also implied, "untaxed on the islands." At least, that is what they inferred. The Republicans, very proud of discovering this loophole, soon herded their ponies to the water's edge and swam them, en masse, over to Assateague. An added bonus was that the island, like any island, is surrounded by water, and ponies shy away from swimming unless forced to do so. Therefore, there was no need to build a fence to corral them, keeping costs low, which appealed directly to these early Republicans' keen sense that money flows in only one direction: towards themselves. But, this version of the pony origin story lacked elegance, and charm. So, someone created a fantastic legend of Spanish galleons to inspire tourists to come see the famous ponies, and perhaps bid on one.

We still can't let go of our romantic notions concerning the ponies. Once a year, about this time, at the end of summer, the Chincoteague fire department rounds up the ancestors of the original untaxed contraband, and forces them to swim across the water in a beautiful tradition that has lasted longer than most of us can remember. The ponies are guided up Pony Swim Lane, trotted through neighborhoods amidst great pomp, ceremony and celebration, like a local Labor Day parade. They end up at the fairgrounds, where they are sold off to the highest bidder and proceeds from the sales keep the town's firetrucks running. An ignominious end to a pony's fabled existence, but arguably a pragmatic ending.

The bugs learned that once a year, humans forced the ponies to swim across the channel. But, it took them a long time to realize that during this event, the Beech 18 doesn't criss-cross the sky to spray insecticide. It seems that no one on the island wants to have a parade under a cloud of poison, or wants to buy a pony coated in a sheen of noxious chemicals. But, the bugs finally figured it out, and in 2016, as the firemen saddled up, billions, perhaps trillions of Moss-Skweetos convened in the air over Assateague. As the firemen rounded up the ponies, the bugs drew up their ranks. When the firemen herded the ponies into the water, the Moss-Skweetos formed a dense cloud just overhead and shadowed the ponies across the channel. They followed them ashore, and then descended upon the neighborhoods where residents and tourists alike swatted at the bugs and complained. They trailed the ponies to the fairgrounds, and there, the bugs steeled themselves to make a final mad dash across Queen Sound channel, over the causeway to Wallops, to swarm the giant parabolic radio telescope.

  Since it was Two for Tuesdays at Don's Seafood Restaurant, and since it was 11:45 am, Darryl drove his car across the causeway still ignorant of the fractured messages the bugs were sending him on the billboards. As he drove the last stretch of road up and over the arched bridge, at the end of the causeway, he immediately saw throngs of tourists clogging the sidewalks and the streets. Darryl groaned, realizing that this year, Two for Tuesdays coincided with the annual pony swim. He considered turning around right there and then to leave the island, but his puppy love for Molly overwhelmed his disdain of crowds.

  Molly leaned against the wall of the waitress station staring longingly at a stolen magazine picture of the Buenos Aires skyline. She imagined herself literally swept off her feet mid-tango by an olive skinned young man who cut a trim figure in tight black pants. His black shirt unbuttoned all the way to his taught belly. His name, she decided, was Manuel. But then, Molly was reluctantly pulled back into Don's Seafood Restaurant reality. She gradually became aware of motion in her periphery. The hostess sat Darryl at his regular table. Molly sighed, set off across the dining room, forcing a smile, knowing good and well that doing so improved the chance of boosting Darryl's ego, and therefore, her tip.

  Darryl pretended not to notice Molly gliding across the room. Instead, he half-gazed out the window across the water at Wallops, and at his monster Extra Terrestrial Telescope, which glowed white in the noontime sun.

Molly sidled up to the table, "Mornin' Luv," she said.

"Hey," Darryl faked surprise.

"The usual?" Molly asked.

"Oh yeah. Sure." Darryl replied.

Molly, ever the professional waitress looking to expand her tip, again employed the tried and true restaurant tactic of small talk. "Going to see the ponies today?"

But Darryl, like the brainiest of engineers, simply couldn't grasp certain elementary concepts of human interaction, like small talk. Plus, he was so smitten by the statuesque woman in front of him, he replied the only way he knew how: tersely.

"No," he said.

Molly smiled a little more genuinely, finding Darryl's naivety sweet. She tapped her pen on her pad and asked, "Have you ever seen the ponies swim?"

"No," Darryl replied.

"Oh, you should luv! Who doesn't love a pony?" Molly didn't.

"Oh yeah, everyone, sure," Darryl said, "Yeah, I should go see them." For a moment Darryl thought that maybe, just maybe, Molly was dropping a hint. She wanted to go see the ponies, and she wanted Darryl to take her there: sort of a date. "Maybe I'll go see them later today," he asserted.

Molly tilted her pen at him and said, "There you go, luv. I know you'll like 'em. Let me know if you buy one, okay?"

Darryl then realized no date was in the offing, but nodded, "I will."

"Yeah." Molly said. "Okay then. I'll be right back with your Crab Imperial!"

"Yeah, thanks," Darryl said, trying to hold a smile.

Molly turned and walked away. Darryl pretended not to watch her lank figure swish and swivel, dancing a slalom among the tables. He pretended not to notice how dark blue her jeans were: so dark they seemed right off the shelf. He pretended not to notice how the deep gold stitching on her pockets accentuated her cheeks, and how they danced with her as she moved. Darryl even pretended not to be disappointed as Molly disappeared behind the wall of the waitress station. He propped his chin in the palm of his hand, his eyes defocused as he did something a tight-sphinctered engineer like him rarely did: he slipped into a daydream...

As Molly walked away, Darryl rushed to his feet and stopped her with a light touch to the shoulder. She turned, and they gazed into each other's eyes, but for a moment. The room darkened and a spotlight illuminated the couple. Darryl thought he could hear angels singing in the distance. His hand slid to the small of her back, and he took her right hand, cradling it within his. Molly delicately placed a caressing hand on his shoulder, and they swirled around the room like Astaire and Rogers. Restaurant patrons and other employees formed a circle around the pair, cheerfully admiring their deep desire for each other. The room melted away, and Darryl and Molly stood outside their new cape cod home, complete with picket fence, well placed flowers and quaint window shutters. A step forward and they were inside, fawning over their two angelic children, a boy and a girl, who were both constructing innovative Rube Goldberg devices from Tinkertoys. Across the room, a little mottled gray cat napped, snuggled on the couch with a Border Collie, who was her best friend. Life was good. Molly leaned close to Darryl, and the two rubbed noses. They were in love. They were content.

Darryl caught himself daydreaming. He realized he had never daydreamed about love or beauty. Before this, his most creative achievement was when his boring, scientific mind assigned colors to numbers. Constructing this fantasy was the most elaborate thing his imagination had ever generated. This was his first inkling that unbridled creativity and expanded awareness could fuel pure, limitless conjecture, as long as he didn't let facts or the truth get in the way. This was an epiphany for Darryl. He felt that if he could now imagine this, he could imagine anything. If he wanted to contemplate the universe, he had only to use his mind. And though, for the first time in his life, it seemed his mind was capable of exploring infinity, Darryl's mind was at the same moment, ironically, wholly unable to fathom the real events that were happening just a few blocks away.

The cloud of bugs hovered over the ponies corralled in the fairgrounds' paddock. The bugs poised to sprint over Queen Sound Channel, to the Extra Terrestrial Telescope. They saw no spray trucks on the roads, and no spray plane in the sky: the path was clear. So the order was given to make the final mad dash for Wallops.

Had Darryl looked out the window instead of pretending he could actually dance, he would have seen the sun darkened by a swarm of bugs. Had he just looked out the window instead of thinking that Molly would ever be satisfied with a cape cod and a picket fence, he would have seen the bugs racing across the channel toward Wallops. Had he looked out the window instead of believing that kids still played with Tinkertoys, he would have seen his gleaming-white, prized telescope blacken as it was blanketed by the bugs. Had Darryl not been so full of himself, and so taken by his newfound imagination, he would have seen pulsating waves sweep from bug to bug, across the surface of the telescope. He would have seen space infinitely curve upon itself, forming a sphere of refracted light that warped and distorted the view of the clouds in the sky. He would have seen a blackness grow from within, like ink in water, that soon revealed stars and planets. Had Darryl been a little more like the old, boring, unimaginative Darryl who saw only reality from the evidence directly in front of him, he would have seen a large crystal ball floating over his telescope: a ball almost half as large as the parabolic dish itself.

Finally, after millennia, the bugs successfully opened a wormhole to home. They beat their collective wings at certain frequencies and wriggled their bodies at designated amplitudes to induce the telescope to generate a radio signal. They focused the radio signal into the wormhole and sent a three part message to their home world, the first and second parts saying, "Here we are. Please send a star cruiser to come and get us."

Here's the deal: a wormhole, as you already know, opens a door to the other side of the universe. Without the wormhole, the bugs' radio message, traveling at the speed of light, would take a billion years to get out of our solar system, out of the galaxy, across the void of space, into the Moss-Skweetos' galaxy, into their solar system, and into their radio receivers. The Chincoteague bugs, after having survived hundreds of millennia on Earth, and after having dealt with idiot humans and all their ancestral iterations for much of that time, were no longer in the mood to suffer fools. They wanted to send their message quickly.

But you ask, why not just fly up into the wormhole and get home that way? Because, it seems, in the end, in a way, they are just bugs, and space is just as inhospitable to their bodies as it is to ours. So, the bugs asked the home world to send a star cruiser to pick them up. And this is why the bugs felt the need to send the third part of their message: "Make sure the wormhole is much larger than a basketball, and keep it open."

The kitchen door swung open and Molly emerged carrying a tray with Darryl's food. Darryl fiddled with his utensils. He sat up in his chair as if he just noticed her. Molly approached and smiled at Darryl, who smiled back. Her eyes were suddenly drawn out the window. She stopped cold in the middle of the room. Molly's smile faded. "What's your telescope doing?" She asked.

Darryl turned and found a large star-filled crystal ball floating above his Extra Terrestrial Telescope, which was covered by what appeared to be undulating bugs. He knew right away that he was witnessing a wormhole—he was a NASA engineer, after all. But, he couldn't explain the bugs.

Had his new found, creative imagination kicked in, Darryl might have surmised that the bugs had used his telescope to create the wormhole. He might have then figured out that the bugs weren't simply bugs, they were something more, something much, much more than he ever imagined them to be. Maybe, just maybe, they were an alien race. And, if they were indeed an alien race, then all the years he spent looking up to the sky for Extra Terrestrial life had simply been a fool's errand.

But instead, Darryl still couldn't muster his new found imagination into action. Wormholes are fantastic creations of the grand universe, and bugs, well, are just bugs. C doesn't follow B, and B, doesn't follow A, therefore, the wormhole and the bugs, are not connected: even though he was directly observing evidence to the contrary.

Darryl turned to Molly, who was standing stone faced in the middle of the room, still holding Darryl's plate of crab imperial. "Check please?" He asked.

Bazoopa zoop zoop

zoopa zoop zoop

zoopa zoop zoop-a

zoopa zoop zoop

    Darryl raced his car out of the parking lot, plowed over the curb, his tires screeching and squealing as he careened through downtown Chincoteague.

Zoopa zoop zoop-a

Zoopa zoop zoop

    He hurtled down the causeway, illegally crossing the double yellow line several times in order to pass slower cars.

Bazoopa zoop zoop-a

zoopa zoop zoop

    Darryl zoomed to the guard station at Wallops, where he frantically demanded that the guard, "open the gate!" He pointed at the wormhole above the telescope and shouted, "OPEN THE GATE!"

The guard looked over his shoulder. He spotted the bugs, but ignorantly overlooked the wormhole. He scrambled to push the button that lifts the gate. "Do you want me to call the spray truck?" He asked, but before he could finish, Darryl sped away. The guard called the spray truck anyway.

Zoop-aaaaa

zoopa zoopa zoopa zoop zoop!

Darryl stopped his car just short of the telescope. He leaned over the dashboard and observed the wormhole and the bugs through the safety of the windshield. He dared not get out of the car. He knew the bugs would be on him in a second. The wormhole warped and bent light inside the sphere. Darryl could make out stars, presumably from another galaxy. He marveled at it all, but still wondered exactly how it all was happening, and why.

Henry stopped the spray truck alongside Darryl's car and tooted its horn, Darryl hardly noticed. Henry honked again and finally got Darryl's attention. He pointed to his own chest, pointed at the bugs on the telescope and then whirled a finger around in the air, like the nozzle of the spray truck.

"Sure." Darryl nodded.

Henry pressed a button and a large on-board air compressor fired up, chugging and hissing. He grabbed a joystick on the dashboard and aimed the nozzles at the bugs on the telescope. He checked the compressor gauge, resting his finger on the joystick trigger, waiting for full pressure. The needle crept almost into the red, and Henry started to squeeze.

But in a flash, the bugs dispersed. They had seen the spray truck arrive. They heard it power up, and watched it aim the nozzle. They had gotten their message through the wormhole, so they quickly peeled off the telescope before Henry could kill them, and then fled back to Assateague.

With the bugs gone, there was nothing left to sustain the wormhole, so it shrank and shrank until it was nothing.

"No!" Darryl yelled. He abandoned his car and stomped around the tarmac. "No, no, no!" And as he watched the wormhole dwindle, Darryl got an idea. He ran into his office and woke his computer to see if it had recorded anything that just happened. To his surprise, it did, and there, on the screen was a squiggly line, jutting up and down like a jagged set of teeth. It was a waveform: amplitude and frequency. It was a signal that could best be described to you and me, as sound.

Darryl clicked here and there on his computer. He opened one program, and then another, in order to analyze the sound. He pushed play, but nothing happened, but then he noticed, that something actually was happening; a high pitch whine, a buzz. In one short burst of actual imagination, Darryl had the idea to transpose the sound down into the realm of human hearing. With one last click he pushed play.

This was what Darryl heard:

Bazoopa zoop zoop

zoopa zoop zoop

zoopa zoop zoop-a

zoopa zoop zoop

Zoopa zoop zoop-a

Zoopa zoop zoop

Bazoopa zoop zoop-a

zoopa zoop zoop

Zoop-aaaaa

zoopa zoopa zoopa zoop zoop!

    At that moment, Darryl became the first human being on Earth to hear a message sent by an alien race. At the same time, he became the first human being to hear an alien race speak in their own language. This might have been the most momentous and historic moment in human history, but Darryl's short lived imagination now failed him.

    He bolted from his desk and poked his head into Dave's office across the hall. Dave, still playing solitaire on his computer, could barely be bothered to notice Darryl standing there.

    "Dave?" Darryl could hardly contain his excitement.

    "Yes?"

"Have you been running anything on the Extra Terrestrial Telescope?"

Dr. Mills often rowed a dingy over to Assateague Island, because it appeared that the conditions there were far more conducive to larger populations of bugs. He'd wander around the island, going south until he could go no further, and then he'd wander to the north until he crossed the imaginary dotted line that delineated Virginia from Maryland. Dr. Mills never seemed to understand that he was crossing an imaginary dotted line. First, because he focused intently when he studied bugs, but more importantly, it was an imaginary dotted line. No one painted a dotted line in the sand, or put up a dotted fence, or even thought to put up a sign saying, "Welcome to Maryland." So how would he have known it was there, or that it wasn't?

Borders used to be less imaginary. Before dotted lines existed, tribes separated themselves with natural barriers, like a river. One tribe would say to another tribe, "That side of the river is yours, this side of the river is ours. You eat from the very limited food supply over there. We'll eat what little we have over here, and that way, neither of us will starve. If you stay on that side of the river, and therefore stay away from our food, we won't kill you. And, we'll stay on this side of the river, to stay away from your food, so you don't kill us. Agreed?"

But then at some point, borders became less about natural barriers that kept us from killing each other over nuts and berries, and became conceptual divisions in the name of travel, and especially commerce. People started drawing lines around the planet to help them find their way to various places. This helped them reach, and remember, the locations of unclaimed real estate: real estate that they could then take for themselves, subdivide with imaginary dotted lines, and then sell to other people. All of a sudden they could say, this is mine, and that is yours, because the dotted line says so. Your money says that over there is yours, and our money says, over here is ours. If you stay on that side of the dotted line we won't kill you, and we'll stay on our side of the dotted line, so you don't kill us. What was, and still is amazing, is that with no proof other than ink on a piece of paper called a map, and ink on another piece of paper called money, people actually agree that these dotted lines exist. We agree on something, that is actually nothing, which makes it something. It's mind boggling, really.

Though the bugs never agreed to, nor acknowledged these borders, the Moss-Skweeto intelligentsia just happened to live and concentrate their efforts and development on Assateague Island, thus staying within natural barriers and imaginary dotted lines. But average bugs, who were dumber and lazier, swarmed to wherever they could find a cozy stagnant puddle to loaf around in and have sex; on Chincoteague, on the Delmarva, on the mainland and eventually beyond, to just about everywhere on the planet. The smart bugs found it particularly easy to inhabit Assateague Island, because it had standing water just about anywhere they looked, even across the imaginary dotted line that divided Virginia and Maryland, which of course, didn't exist to them. They liked it there because people largely left them alone, except for Dr. Mills, who covered himself with mud and wandered the marshes and beaches scribbling gentlemanly observations in his leather bound notebook about the bugs Elijah James called "Mosquitoes."

After a few years, Dr. Mills felt satisfied with his research. He washed the protective mud from his skin, put on nice, clean clothes again and left Chincoteague on a row boat across Queen Sound Channel to the Delmarva. He reassured himself it had been worth all the effort. He had filled his leather bound notebook with countless observations, drawings and inscriptions. He later presented his findings to academia in his dissertation, "Chincoteague Mosquitoes." His colleagues patted him on the back as they all celebrated with cigars and small glasses of moderately priced sherry. History would later credit Dr. Mills with creating the word "mosquito," even though he first heard the word spoken by Elijah James. And though Dr. Mills was still not officially an entomologist, because that word still had not been created yet, he was officially an etymologist, even though he actually wasn't.

The word "mosquito" has become so commonplace that we now hardly notice it, and we casually wave it off like, well, like a tiny mosquito hovering at the end of our nose. It means so little to us, because we don't realize what it actually means, because Elijah James told Dr. Mills the wrong word. Plus, the word "mosquito" is insignificant on its own. It needs a larger context for us to even take notice, like a swarm of mosquitoes attacking our eyes and our ears and our nostrils. Amazingly, sometimes even that doesn't work.

When the townsfolk and tourists of Chincoteague first saw the sphere over Wallops, they stopped whatever they were doing: walking on the sidewalk, riding a rented bike, fishing from the docks. They then gawked at the thing floating over the Extra Terrestrial Telescope. They couldn't believe their eyes, or they wouldn't believe their eyes, even though proof was as obvious as a swarm of mosquitoes right in front of them, which there actually was.

When it was all over, the entire town was ablaze with chatter.

"What was it?" A child asked her father, as both ate soft serve on the patio of Mr. Whippy.

"Just a NASA experiment, dear." He assured her, like fathers do, when they don't know what they're talking about.

"Them engineers are at it again!" said the hostess at Don's looking across the parking lot. "They're always blowing up stuff over there." Then she added, "A waste of money. I'm going to stop paying my taxes."

"It's nothing," said an old fisherman to his grandson, who was emptying a crab pot, "swamp gas."

The old couple pedaled their rented bikes down Main Street. The old man turned to the old lady and quietly asked, "Is that in the guide book?"

People clambered around town frantically looking for an answer to that thing they saw floating in the sky. If the answer had been a tiny mosquito hovering at the end of their nose, they could be forgiven for not noticing it. But, the answer was a billion bugs peeling off the telescope, flying over their heads in one concerted black cloud towards Assateague. Still, no one, no one, paid the slightest attention to them. To be fair, no one on Earth had ever seen a wormhole floating in the air over their town before. Since no average person knew a word for that thing, it didn't exist in their minds, which of course, made them all the more curious about it.

In contrast, bugs were bugs. The people of Chincoteague didn't know to pay attention to the bugs. To the islanders, they were common every day mosquitoes, not alien Moss-Skweetos. If they had known the word "Moss-Skweeto," the right word for the bugs, they would have known to think about the bugs differently. They would have known that words mean stuff, which in turn gives meaning to stuff. They might have even rightly surmised that the bugs were responsible for the wormhole. But, they didn't. They had no curiosity about the mosquitoes whatsoever, because it turns out that all along they had been using a slightly wrong word for a thing, which in essence, made it a different thing. Then to obfuscate the Moss-Skweetos real existence even further, at one point, they chose to call a bug, their official bird. No wonder.

Molly mindlessly drove across the causeway toward the Delmarva. It had been a long day. She was forced to work her entire shift, even after witnessing one of the most amazing and perplexing things anyone on the island had ever seen. People had heard about the sphere, and came to the waterfront to get a look for themselves. While they were there, people got hungry, so Don's took advantage of this new opportunity and stayed open late. Though Molly benefitted from extra tips, from extra customers, she resented this new opportunity.

Behind the wheel, she tried to lose herself in a daydream, but couldn't. Instead, she stared at the empty backsides of the billboards, all of which faced traffic coming to the island (why advertise to someone leaving the island?). Back on the Delmarva, she spotted Darryl's giant telescope through her bug splatted windshield. Huge spotlights flooded the giant dish and the area around it, almost blinding Molly as she passed by. Official looking people clustered at its base, many of them inspecting the telescope very closely. She wondered if Darryl was among them.

Tired, done with work, and faced with yet another boring night of waiting to do it all over again, Molly opened the front door of her rented trailer on the swampy Delmarva lot. She was met by the sight of bald Lucas sprawled on the couch, watching TV, still in his Burger Chef uniform, looking like a lounging hamburger. Molly groaned.

"I told you not to wear that thing on the couch."

Lucas' eyes never left the TV, "You did." He said.

"Ugh! You're getting french fry grease all over it!"

"Hmm," he grunted.

"What if we want to trade it up towards a better couch?" She asked.

"What if we don't?"

"Arrghh!" Molly growled, stomping into the kitchen. She threw her pocketbook onto the counter, leaned on the backrest of one of their two rented chairs and glared into the other room at Lucas. He was watching a PBS program about the Chesapeake Bay, specifically, one of those programs filmed from the air in the best morning or evening light, showcasing the stunning beauty of a given landscape. All of this while a narrator poetically describes what the viewer is already looking at. Occasionally, a semi-famous actor reads a passage by a semi-famous author that even more poetically describes what the viewer is already looking at. Molly honestly didn't understand what drew Lucas to this TV show.

Molly cocked an angry hip, "You know that's like ten minutes away from here."

"Yep," Lucas replied.

"You could just drive there and see it for yourself. You could probably ride your bike there."

"Or I can watch it on TV."

Molly rolled her eyes and stomped into the TV room where she pleaded with Lucas, "Let's go somewhere."

"We are somewhere."

"Somewhere else."

"Where?"

"Anywhere." She argued.

"How about the bay? It's on TV right now."

"You know what I mean."

"I do know what you mean, but right now, I'm watching TV!"

"TV sucks!" Molly asserted. "Don't you want to go someplace real?"

"Yeah."

"Really? Where?"

"This very real couch."

"Gawd!" Molly threw up her hands, "Let's go to the mountains. We could stay in a cozy little mountaintop cabin. We could get up really early and lounge on the front porch: sip coffee, look at dewdrops on the grass, and fog in the valleys. It would be so beautiful, so different. "

"Or we could sleep in," Lucas sneered, "preferably on this couch."

"We could go to Baltimore or Philly, and stay downtown in a high rise hotel. That would be so exciting."

"Exciting is stressful, and expensive."

"You just don't want to go anywhere." Molly barked.

Lucas finally took his eyes off the TV, turned and leaned in toward Molly, "YOU...ARE...CORRECT!" He sunk back into the couch cushions, and stared at the TV again.

Molly groaned, stormed out the front door and plopped down on the stoop. She surveyed her miserable swampy yard, her two hundred dollar K car, and her crappy life, with nearly as much disdain as she now had for Lucas. She brought her knees to her chin, hugged her legs and tried to lose herself in the night sky. Straight up, the stars sparkled brilliantly against inky blackness. She thought about how impossibly far away they must be from Earth, and how unreachable they were by someone like her. Molly's eyes drifted down toward the horizon, and the black sky awash with a milky light pollution from the nearby floodlights at Wallops. Just above the treetops, Molly could make out the very tip top of Darryl's big telescope. It suddenly became obvious that the sphere would have been in full view from her stoop, and so much closer than what she saw from Don's Seafood Restaurant. Perhaps she could have seen details inside the sphere that would have been indiscernible from the island. Details that would have explained the big ball in the sky. But then, she dismissed that notion. She was just a lousy high school dropout: a failure. What would she know? Molly decided to just ask Darryl about the sphere the next time she saw him. He is a NASA guy after all. It is his telescope, his job.

Darryl should know all about it, and he did, though at the same time, he didn't. For the next few hours, Molly sat alone on the front stoop, wondering about stuff here on the planet, and stuff out there, off the planet, and what it all meant.

The next morning, Molly struggled to get her act together. She was late for work. She rummaged around the trailer, frantic and exasperated. Lucas walked out of the bedroom dressed for his shift at the Burger Chef. He watched as Molly bounced around the room upturning pillows on the couch, and searching under stacks of stolen magazines on the coffee table.

He lifted the tail of his shirt and scratched his belly. "What?" he asked.

"I can't find my keys," she complained.

"Look on the counter," he said.

"They're not on the counter," she groused.

"Behind the chips," Lucas said.

Molly, loathing that Lucas might actually be right, dashed to the counter and discovered her keys under a half eaten bag of potato chips.

"Gottem," she said.

"I know," he answered.

She raced to the front door, whisking past Lucas.

"Not even a goodbye?" He asked.

Molly turned around to face him, and there he was, standing there in his Burger Chef uniform: a big, walking, polyester hamburger. It took only a moment for Molly to think back just a short time ago, in high school; Lucas swaggered down the halls in expensive-looking cowboy boots, black jeans and chrome studded black jean jacket. He was one of the few guys in high school who could grow a full beard, and did. His lank hair dangled around his shoulders, his musky, unwashed aroma permeated his very being and everything within smelling distance. The very sight of him excited her.

That image of Lucas faded into a slightly older, balder, man. The studded jean jacket seemed a little too small for his now paunchy frame, and his belly hung over the belt of skinny jeans that were embarrassingly tight. The boots, well they just looked wrong on a guy who looked older than his actual age.

That image also faded away, and there again, in front of Molly stood Lucas, the big, bald, hairy-backed, walking polyester hamburger.

"Bye," she said.

The whole town coalesced in Waterfront Park; residents, tourists and transients alike, to see if another sphere would form over Darryl's big telescope. The park, it just so happens, had the best unobstructed view over Queen Sound Channel, and the telescope at Wallops. People packed the parking lot at Don's Seafood Restaurant next door. Many made an excuse to have an exceptionally long lunch on the second floor of Don's, even squatting at Darryl's regular table, so they could look out the window in case something happened. Those who hadn't seen the sphere the first time, had heard about it, and those folks rushed to the waterside so they wouldn't miss it again, if it actually happened again. They all stood in the park cheek to jowl, jostling for the best position for the best view. Those who couldn't worm their way dockside, stood on picnic tables under the pavilion, on the oversized Adirondack chairs that spelled "LOVE," on the steps of the library, on any raised surface they could find. They even climbed on the statue of Misty. No one at the park understood that the thing that had hovered over Darryl's telescope was a wormhole, they just knew that it wasn't normal. They all figured that those smarty pants over at NASA were probably up to something big. But as you and I already know, this assumption was wrong: the Moss-Skweetos were up to something big. The smarty pants at NASA were almost as clueless as everyone else.

Darryl inspected his computer screen and saw no new squiggly lines indicating anything unusual. There were actually no squiggly lines at all on the screen, definitively indicating that nothing unusual was happening. Darryl was perplexed. A wasn't resulting in B, which wasn't leading to C, and so on. He knew there had been a wormhole over his Extra Terrestrial Telescope: he had seen it himself. He just couldn't figure out how it got there. He went from room to room at Wallops and asked each person if they had done anything to create a wormhole over the telescope. Each time they shrugged or just stared blankly at him. Dave, on the other hand peered at Darryl over his half moon readers, chuckled derisively, and again verified with absolute certainty that, "no, it wasn't me," and went back to playing solitaire on his computer.

Before long, everyone at the facility, except Dave, were scrambling to understand what had happened. Like Darryl, many looked at their computer screens for answers, but just as many simply walked outside and gawked at the telescope: as if doing so would produce results. Darryl eventually gave up on seeing anything happen on his computer. He left the building to join the other gawkers at the base of the telescope. They milled about postulating causes: a rogue scientist at Wallops, an alien race opened the wormhole from across the universe, a naturally occurring phenomenon, or even swamp gas. Darryl stared in disbelief. He stroked his chin. He asked himself a simple question, and he happened to be the only scientist in the crowd to ask this simple question, "what was different before, when the wormhole was open?" It happened to be the right question to ask.

    He paced and paced. He tried to make C follow B, and B follow A, but he could never come to a logical conclusion as to the actual cause of the wormhole. He glanced at the telescope again, and was blinded by sunlight reflecting off of the gleaming white surface. When the wormhole floated over Wallops; A – the telescope wasn't gleaming. Why? B – is was covered in bugs, blocking the sun's reflections, with the exception of the sheen from their beating wings. C – The next logical step would be, well, Darryl couldn't imagine what the next logical step would be. He was genuinely stumped, even though he was directly facing the answer, or more accurately, that he wasn't. He inspected his forearm arm: no bugs, no bites. He rubbed his neck and face; no blood, no welts, no bugs.

    "Huh," he said to himself. He looked around. None of the other scientist were swatting at the air, nor were they swatting at any creatures on their own arms. Darryl asked, "Where are all of the bugs?" This was also the right question to ask, but asking the right question, doesn't always lead to the right answer. Darryl stared blankly at the telescope.

That's all anyone at Waterfront Park could do: stare at the telescope. The crowd milled about impatiently, every eyeball in the crowd glued to Wallops, focused like they had never focused before in their life. Everyone wanted so badly to see a show over at Wallops, that no one noticed that not a single person in the park swatted a bug or waved one off. They didn't notice that not one person there was bothered or bitten by a bug. And, no one noticed the complete absence of even one tiny little bug at Waterfront Park, because like an imaginary dotted line, it's hard to notice what isn't there.

Molly drove her two hundred dollar K car passed Wallops in a hurry, and observed the group of scientists and engineers gathered around Darryl's telescope. She thought she glimpsed Darryl, but Molly didn't have time to slow down and make sure. Molly wondered about the sphere over Wallops, but could wonder only so much: she had to get to work. She had to make money to pay for all the crappy stuff she rented. Her car rounded a crook in the road and she raced down the causeway. Molly largely ignored the billboards and the subliminal images imbedded in them by John James, who at the moment was pasting up another ad. As Molly approached Chincoteague, she saw the large crowd packed into Waterfront Park and Don's parking lot. Her first thought was not, "what's happening?" or, "what are all of those people doing over there?" Her first thought was, "great, now where am I gonna park?" She groaned, rolled her eyes and pressed the gas a little harder. She didn't want to be too late for work, even though she really didn't want to be at work at all.

And then, over the heads of the crowd at Waterfront Park, Molly saw a glimmer in the sky. Or maybe it was a shimmer. In the far distance behind the crowd, the sky swirled. Space infinitely curved upon itself, forming a sphere of refracted light that warped and distorted the view of the clouds in the blue sky. Suddenly, a large crystal ball floated over Assateague Island. It was much bigger than a basketball. Molly slowed down, almost stopping on the causeway. A blackness grew from within the sphere, like ink spreading in water. She could just make out stars, and what looked like a planet.

Molly eased onto Chincoteague, passing Don's and all the people in Waterfront Park with barely a thought or second glance. She pressed the accelerator and raced through town trying to maintain visual contact with the sphere. It came in and out of sight between houses and through stands of tall pine trees. She barreled through the entrance of Assateague wildlife refuge and sped down the road until she reached the beach where the Spanish ponies never came ashore. It was as far as she could go. It was as far as anyone could go. It was the farthest place in the upper right hand corner of Virginia, where the ocean pushes froth up on the yellow sand beach. Molly careened into a public parking lot where she stopped, and hopped out of her car, carelessly leaving the door swinging open.

"Huh," she whispered. She shuffled toward the crystal ball hovering over the beach. Molly perceived a twinge tweaking the spider web tattoo on her neck. A bug was biting her. She mindlessly swatted it.

Darryl paced. He impatiently paced some more. He paced and paced. The other scientists gathered around the telescope paced and paced with him, but still nothing happened. Hyper intelligent NASA scientists and engineers, smart enough to fully understand that pacing over and over can't open a wormhole, paced and paced, like maybe it could.

At 10:01 a.m. a door opened on the side of the massive NASA building. Dave, always fastidious, had closed his computer game of solitaire and was now about to take his morning walk around the facility. He stepped out the door and was a little embarrassed to find himself face to face with a large group of NASA scientists pacing beneath the telescope. He had been so engrossed in solitaire that he never noticed that he was alone inside the building. Dave, feeling a little exposed, nervously nodded and began to take a lap around the facility. But, he took only a step, when over the heads of Darryl and everyone else, and far behind them, he noticed a glimmer in the sky. Or, maybe it was a shimmer. Before he knew it, a large crystal ball floated over Assateague Island. Although Dave spent all of his time flying his desk, playing solitaire, caring only enough to ride out the time clock to the end of the day and eventually to retirement, he was still, in fact, a NASA scientist. And Dave knew that he was now looking at a wormhole.

"Guys," he said, but no one paid attention to him, because no one ever paid attention to him anymore. Dave pointed at the sky above Assateague and shouted, "Guys!"

One scientist heard him and turned to where he pointed. She saw the wormhole and then nudged another colleague to look. One by one they turned toward the sphere, and a hush fell over the crowd.

Finally, Darryl also turned to see what everyone was looking at.

"Huh," he said.

All of the very smart NASA scientists and engineers stood there for a few moments, dumfounded. Darryl broke from the crowd, scurried to his car, bolted to the exits and raced toward the wormhole floating over Assateague. His fellow scientist and engineers followed suit, except for Dave, who finished his lap around the building and returned to his desk for more solitaire.

A few people at Waterfront Park heard the faint whine of car engines on the causeway. They watched curiously as a caravan of cars sped toward the island. More people took notice as the caravan approached, the whine of their engines becoming a growl. The cars crossed onto the island and blew through town like a presidential motorcade. Everyone at Waterfront Park were keenly interested. Mahesh Venkatachalam, who was in the park with his family reveling in all things Chincoteague, was the first one in the crowd to notice the sphere over on Assateague.

"Huh," he said, now understanding where the cars were headed.

"Guys," he said, but no one heard him. He pointed at the sky above Assateague and shouted, "Guys!"

One by one, everyone turned to see what he was pointing at, and then they saw the sphere. In a flash everyone rushed to their cars, or their mopeds, or their rented bikes, and raced to Assateague.

Bazoopa zoop zoop

zoopa zoop zoop

zoopa zoop zoop-a

zoopa zoop zoop

Zoopa zoop zoop-a

Zoopa zoop zoop

Bazoopa zoop zoop-a

zoopa zoop zoop

Zoop-aaaaa

zoopa zoopa zoopa zoop zoop!

    Molly staggered closer to the wormhole. It was larger than the one floating over Darryl's telescope. It was far larger than the wormhole that opened in low Earth orbit millennia ago, much larger than a basketball actually, though, how could Molly know this? The stars inside grew more brilliant; the planet inside more vivid. Nebulas within the sphere refracted light just so, making them look like, blue powder, like Tang or ocre rouge, suspended in a solution. She was mesmerized by the distant star field's simple beauty and its inconceivable complexity. She was amazed that of all places, it was here, on this dull bug infested island where Virginia ended, in this particular direction. Molly circled the crystal ball. It seemed so far away, but also, so close. She hopped up to touch it with her fingertips, but she couldn't reach it: it was farther away than it seemed. And then she wondered, "Is there a surface you can touch? What if my fingers went straight through to the other side and touched the stars?" Molly retracted her hand and cradled it close to her chest.

A wash of prismatic colors suddenly billowed from within, filling the sphere; red, blue, yellow, orange, green, white. They spiraled and flowed amorphously together like oil on the surface of water, and then, they separated and became distinct primary colors. They filled the sphere, and Molly stepped back. A Moss-Skweeto star cruiser then emerged from the wormhole. It was different than the first one that crash-landed on Earth millennia ago. It was bigger, about the size of a giant beach ball. Its glossy metal surface was pristinely smooth and divided by distinct longitudinal lines that ran from pole to pole, each delineating a color; red, blue, yellow, orange, green, white, which made the ship look even more like a giant beach ball. It was a rescue ship, designed to carry the stranded Moss-Skweetos back to the home world.

This time, however, the Moss-Skweeto mission control back on the home world opened and controlled the wormhole. And this time, the hole was much larger than the ship, providing a larger door for the ship to pass through, and therefore, providing a greater margin for error. Most importantly, the wormhole stayed open. It didn't shrink and close up, biting off the tail end of the rescue ship, leaving its brakes floating in space on the other side of the universe. And, the wormhole remained open, so the ship could return home when it was good and ready to do so. The message the bugs sent the day before had been heard loud and clear by the home world, and after a millennia, it seems, the Moss-Skweetos on the home world had learned their lesson.

The Moss-Skweeto rescue ship floated silently above the parking lot. The only sounds Molly could hear were small waves gently sloshing onto the beach. Sometimes she also heard the beating of her own heart. The ship placidly rotated in place, a polished spinning beach ball.

Darryl and the NASA caravan sped into the parking lot, skidding to a halt. The scientists and engineers stopped short of the two spheres hanging in the air above the beach. They slowly got out of their cars and cautiously approached. Darryl saw Molly, alone under the spheres, circling them, inspecting them, apparently completely unafraid of something Darryl thought clearly deserved at least a healthy aversion. Darryl shouted across the parking lot, "Molly! Step back!" He yelled, but he was far enough away that the din of the surf drowned him out. Molly never heard him. If she had, she probably would have ignored him, because let's face it, the strange spheres in the sky were far more interesting than Darryl ever was. The rest of the town then filed in and gathered behind the NASA scientists. Many got out of their cars, many stayed in, but they all gawked in disbelief, and unlike Molly, they kept their distance.

Behind them, a dense black cloud rose from the pine forest near the lighthouse: the swamp where the Chincoteague bugs found safe haven from humans. A high pitch whine grew louder.

Molly turned toward the noise, "Bugs," she said. The swarm headed straight toward her, but she soon figured out that she was entirely wrong. She looked up at the beach ball and back at the swarm. They weren't coming toward her. It was at that very point, that after millennia, Molly became the first person on the planet Earth to understand that mosquitoes were not just evil little blood sucking bugs. Neither Darryl nor the other extremely smart NASA scientists across the parking lot, all of whom spent their life's work thinking about incomprehensible things in ways the rest of us don't, had yet to figure out what Molly now knew.

The rescue ship ceased rotation. A hatch opened from the middle of the glassy green segment. Molly witnessed several Moss-Skweetos flying out of the ship and hover around the hatch, like a welcoming committee. The swarm swiftly approached.

Darryl now saw the open hatch. He then saw the approaching swarm. He looked back at the open hatch, and looked back at the approaching swarm. It was at that very point that Darryl became the second person on Earth to understand that mosquitoes were not just evil little blood sucking bugs.

"Oh," he whimpered.

The swarm formed methodically into an orderly column as the Moss-Skweetos at the hatch moved aside. The column then filed into the rescue ship. Molly, awestruck by it all, wondered what would happen when they all were in the ship. Would it just leave, and would that be it? Would she just watch it travel back through the wormhole, across the entire unexplored universe free from the divisions and self-imposed constraints of imaginary dotted lines? What would she then do? Get back into her two hundred dollar K car, drive back to her crappy little job and then have to explain why she was late, all so she could keep a job she didn't want? She'd have to go steal more magazines from beauty salons, cut out pictures of the universe and paste them to the wall of the waitress station. She'd have to stand there and stare at those pictures, wondering what could have been: wishing she was anywhere but where she was. Then she'd have to live every day with the fact that she had just witnessed a spaceship and space aliens, who were going pretty much everywhere but where she was. And then, after all of that, she'd go home to her crappy little rented trailer parked on a swampy little lot. She'd go inside and plop down on her crappy little rented couch and wait for her bald, walking polyester hamburger of a boyfriend to come home, just so she can again face all the same regrets tomorrow, and the day after that, and so on.

Molly contemplated her Dad; how he bought her lunch when she needed a little help. It wasn't much, except that it was. She imagined him as a lonely old man with no one to care for, no one to buy lunch. What would happen to him? She remembered her Mom, standing at the door, unable to make eye contact with her own six year old daughter before vanishing forever. She now understood her Mom, and she now understood herself a little better.

Molly shouted at the bugs, "Hey!"

She waved her arms over her head and shouted again, "Hey!"

Molly's actions perplexed Darryl, "What are you...," he asked under his breath. "Hey!" He shouted, trotting towards her. "No!" He said, "Whatever you're doing..."

A few members of The Moss-Skweeto welcoming committee heard Molly, and flew over to see what she wanted.

Molly, nose to nose with the bugs, said only one thing, "Can I go with you?"

The Moss-Skweeto welcoming committee hovered for a few seconds. They considered her request. They considered her words. They inferred that she meant exactly what she said, and that she didn't imply anything, except exactly what she said. They concluded that words do mean stuff and that in some extremely rare occasions, everybody involved actually agrees that the words mean exactly the same thing. This was one of those rare occasions. An order was given and the column of bugs slowed and slowed until it stopped mid-air. The flow of bugs then redirected toward Molly.

Darryl now sprinted, "No," he shouted. The other NASA scientists, embarrassed and ashamed to have taken so long to fully understand the situation, ran after him.

Molly stood there calm and resolute, as one by one, the bugs landed on her arms, her legs, her body and her head. Millions, perhaps billions, of bugs soon blanketed her body. She heard yelling over her shoulder, so she turned. It was Darryl. He could still see her face, which was rapidly disappearing behind a layer of bugs. Molly managed a soft smile for Darryl. He ran and ran. One of Molly's blue eyes took a last look through the bugs at Darryl, and then in a moment, not a millimeter of Molly was exposed. Darryl stopped, out of breath and shocked to see the shape of a beautiful young woman encrusted by bugs. In the next instant, the bugs dispersed, floating wisps in the air, and Molly was gone. Just gone. No one knew if the bugs had used special powers to load Molly into the ship so she could explore the universe, or if she had just been a convenient snack before they hit the road. No one has ever bothered to ask these questions aloud, because no one really wanted to know.

The column reformed and the bugs boarded the rescue ship. The hatch closed. The ship spun on its axis once again, and floated silently into the wormhole, which then simply closed behind it. Waves crashed on the beach while virtually the whole town tried to grasp what had just happened. Everyone looked around at each other, and then everyone looked at Darryl, standing alone across the parking lot, staring pitifully at the blank sky where the wormhole had been. We didn't know at the time, but Darryl, in one stroke of utter disappointment, became painfully aware that he had overlooked and entire alien race right in his back yard, and at the same moment, he lost the woman he so desperately wanted to love. Darryl slouched and then slogged back through the crowd toward his car. He couldn't muster the strength to look at anyone, as they quietly, awkwardly watched him drive away. No one knew what to do next, so everyone just got into their own cars and slowly drove off.

The parking lot by the beach was then empty except for my family and me, Mahesh Venkatachalam, your narrator. I couldn't help but smile. Chincoteague was every bit as exotic as I imagined it would be. It was a beautiful far-off land with interesting people and an amazing set of stories, whether they are true, or not. The island did not, and does not disappoint. As a matter of fact, Chincoteague, this wonderfully quirky place, is the very reason I gave up my own lucrative career as a confectionary scientist, just to become a storyteller on the island. I'd have it no other way.

At Don't Seafood Restaurant, a ukelele plays:

Chincoteague bugs
Chincoteague bugs
packin' up their bags and leavin' in a huff

fed up with man
his schemin' and lies
turnin' on the rockets, and headin' for the skies

So long, noble little Chincoteague bugs

The Moss-Skweetos didn't take all of the bugs home. They left the stupid, indolent ones behind on Earth, because they didn't want them, and felt we deserved them. Arrogantly, we still don't think of them as an alien race, and when they bite us, which they still do, we continue to smack them and kill them as if they're just bugs.

NASA was sorely disappointed that Darryl never accomplished his task of discovering an alien race, but at the same time, they also quietly ignored the fact that neither had they.

One discovery Darryl actually made at Wallops flight facility was that at the very back of the property, there was a small, seldom used gate. This gate displayed a perfectly good, though mostly irrelevant rusty metal sign that read "exit." Darryl's boss encouraged him to use it. But that wasn't the end of Darryl on the islands at the upper right hand corner of Virginia. Occasionally you can still find him neatly dressed in his United States park ranger uniform, harassed by a cloud of bugs, cleaning pit toilets over on Assateague. And sometimes, Darryl bitterly regrets that he squandered his amazing career, or he pines over a love that wasn't, and probably could or would never have been, and he feeds his regrets by drowning his sorrows, right over there at the corner of the bar... Sorry Darryl. If I'd known you were here tonight, I'd have told another story—if, that is, I had another story to tell.

CPSIA information can be obtained
at www.ICGtesting.com
Printed in the USA
LVHW052247060721
692003LV00012B/1715